Jacques Chessex (1934–2009) was one of Switzerland's greatest authors, a novelist, poet and essayist. He is revered in France and won the Prix Goncourt in 1973 for *The Tyrant* (*L'Ogre* in the original). His other works include *Monsieur* (2001), *L'Économie du ciel* (2003), *Le Vampire de Ropraz* (2007) and *Un Juif pour l'exemple* (2009), all published in numerous languages. Bitter Lemon Press has published the last two in English as *The Vampire of Ropraz* and *A Jew Must Die*.

D0591660

Other Bitter Lemon books
by Jacques Chessex:

The Vampire of Ropraz
A Jew Must Die

THE TYRANT

Jacques Chessex

Translated by Martin Sokolinsky

BITTER LEMON PRESS
LONDON

BITTER LEMON PRESS

First published in the United Kingdom in 2012 by
Bitter Lemon Press, 37 Arundel Gardens, London W11 2LW

www.bitterlemonpress.com

First published in French as *L'Ogre* by
Bernard Grasset, Paris in 1973

© Éditions Grasset & Fasquelle, 1973
English translation © Martin Sokolinsky, 2012

A CIP record for this book is available from the British Library

ISBN 978–1–904738–94–7

Typeset by Tetragon
Printed and bound by CPI Group (UK) Ltd, Croydon, CR0 4YY

The Tyrant

How long wilt thou not depart from me?

Job 7:19

Contents

Part I
The Crematorium

Let me alone; for my days are vanity.

Job 7:16

IT WAS EVENING WHEN his torment began.

At first he felt strangely alone seated before the dinner that he had just ordered in the bar of the Hôtel d'Angleterre. At the other tables people were laughing; radiant, tanned women spoke to handsome men. Young couples held hands. Tense, gloomy, Jean Calmet carefully shifted three fillets of perch in his plate; once again he sprinkled them with lemon, then his fork pushed one little fish, drolly lining it up ironically against the two others; but he could not make up his mind to bring it to his mouth. The wine in his glass grew lukewarm. For an hour he had been persecuted by an image. Jean Calmet hesitated to look at it; he pushed it away, he buried it in the opaque layers of his memory; because he knew that he was going to suffer the moment he allowed it to come into focus. But the blurred image surfaced again, it persisted, and now Jean Calmet could no longer ignore it, against the background of shadows that made it even clearer. Suddenly his loneliness became unbearable and the whole picture emerged.

It was a very old scene, one that had taken place thousands of times when he lived with his family in Lutry, beside the lake, in a house shattered by angry shouts, in the lee of the poplars and firs. They were seated for the evening meal. The father, immense, presided at the head of the table. The light of the setting sun reddened his shining, gilded forehead; his thick arms also shone with orange light; his innate strength was apparent: the muscles and solid flesh of his chest stretched the shirt, exposing a forest of grey hair between the nipples that made two points under the cotton. Around him, the room seemed plunged in darkness. But in front of the shadows, which rose from the floor and from the farthest corners of the big room, there was that compact, illuminated mass, that other sun, infallible and detestable, which turned red, which shone, which irradiated itself with all its power.

Seated at the other end of the table, Jean Calmet listened with repugnance to the mouth noises of his father, who was busy eating. Those hissing, sucking sounds disgusted him like a vile confession. Little was said; the brothers and sisters observed one another; the mother ate very quickly, getting up continually, scurrying from the kitchen to the dining room, a frightened grey mouse. Martha, the German-Swiss housekeeper, stared at her plate with a reproachful look. The doctor chewed and swallowed without stopping, but his implacable gaze fell on each member of his family; it ran up and down over the diners, and Jean Calmet grew desperate at the thought of being transfixed once more by those all-powerful eyes which searched him and guessed everything. Under their blue fire he became livid; suddenly he would feel transparent, completely disarmed, unable to conceal anything at all from those terrible pupils. The doctor knew everything about him; the doctor read him like a book, because he was the master, and the master was thick, massive, impenetrable in his strength, compact and florid in the evening sun.

Shame and despair stabbed Jean Calmet's heart. His father knew his larval desires. He knew where the gluey handkerchiefs were hidden. He saw everything at a single glance. Jean Calmet lowered his eyes over his plate without being able to escape the inquisitor. Sadness gripped his throat and he felt like throwing his arms around the old man's neck, crying out all the tears in his body on that broad and sonorous chest. For Jean Calmet loved his father. He loved him, he loved that massive, watchful strength. He despised and envied that appetite, he loved that domineering voice at the same time as he feared it. A rather cowardly fear prevented him from running to the doctor, from snuggling into his arms. This cowardice shamed him like a betrayal.

Supper long over, the doctor drank his coffee noisily without anyone daring to get up. The maid busied herself on tiptoe. Finally, they lit the lamps: that was the signal. After a quick goodnight, everyone went rushing out of the dining room and fled to hide in their rooms as in a secret burrow. But Jean Calmet did not recover from the ordeal. He had the impression that the eyes of his judge followed him, scrutinized him through the walls. Late in the evening, he would still be looking for a refuge or distraction in his books. He went to bed. If he yielded to his desires, his every fibre grew tense at the thought that his father was going to surprise him – even worse, that he had seen him, that he was observing him.

He was fifteen. At that time, he committed little thefts to try to diminish the power of that gaze. To strengthen himself with a secret. He would go into a bookshop; he would browse with a wise, casual look. All of a sudden he would pocket the collection of poetry or the magazine, and he would be out on the street again with a feeling of weight, of solidity, that protected him from his father. At last he had somewhere of his own; a place removed, a place hidden from the censor. But Jean Calmet loved his father. Why had he not told him so? Tears filled the eyes of Jean Calmet, whose mind was blank for a moment. Then he began to eat his cold fish and did his best to get hold of himself by taking his bearings. I'm thirty-eight years old, he said to himself. I'm a schoolmaster at the Gymnase. Sixty rascals think through me. But remembering those teenagers did not cheer him up; on the contrary, he felt too lonely, too strangely afflicted to pretend to give them the least example, to recommend anything whatsoever to them. The wine did not cheer him either. He paid his bill and left to shut himself up at home.

He went to bed but could not fall asleep. That morning's ceremony came back to him. The sense of deliverance that he had felt at the crematorium tortured him like remorse. Following the advice he had read in magazines, he worked hard at letting his body and limbs go limp, abandoning any control by his will; he was about to give himself up to the first sensation of peace when he thought: I'm playing dead. All at once, his pain was revived. He saw again the cemetery of the Bois-de-Vaux, the straight lanes, the thousands of graves. At the bottom of each pit lay a skeleton, a body in a state of decomposition, rudimentarily preserved, the shape of the man it had been. The "last sleep" retained the familiarity of good and simple habit by which one perceived, ridiculously, death's meagre power. There was something reassuring about it, something seen before, which pierced Jean Calmet's heart. The grave was like a daily bed. Those bones endured. The skull, the teeth, the fractures, the size of the body were perfectly recognizable; dentist's fillings, rings, shreds of clothing could be identified. This kind of purely physical survival suddenly seemed to Jean Calmet as precious as eternity. And he, what had he done with his father? What had his brothers and sisters decided? What had they made him agree to? To hear them, there was nothing so filthy as that corpse rotting under a few inches of earth. They had to think of Mother. The image of the doctor in decomposition would pursue her without respite. And what of public health? They were having a particularly warm autumn. An added reason. In this kind of weather the dead rot faster. With relief, Jean Calmet approved. The doctor would be reduced to ashes. He could not be allowed any chance of keeping his exasperating, scandalous vigour in the fertile earth. That strength, those muscles, had to be destroyed, right down to those eyes, the thick red lids of which had been shut uselessly for a few hours. Destroy his father. Make a little heap of ashes of him, ashes at the bottom of an urn. Like sand. Anonymous, mute dust. Blind sand.

And now Jean Calmet was torn at the thought of that urn. Where would it be kept? It was possible that his mother might want to keep it near her. The mortuary representative had ceremoniously warned them, him and his brothers: the widow might demand to keep the ashes in her garden, in her living room, or even at her bedside, so as not to be separated from her beloved. At the time, Jean Calmet had smiled inwardly, touched by such superstitious loyalty. Now that he was living in the moist darkness, tired out by his heavy sheets, the memory of the mortician's words began to trouble him, obsess him: did the naive wish of these women stem from a deep, magical intuition, one which conferred on the recipient and its meagre contents the terrifying quality of human presence? Thus, through the simplicity of doting old ladies, the remains – which he had believed so totally devoid of power – took on evil importance again. No, it was better to convince himself that this miserable handful of cinders was harmless. Sweepings. Jean Calmet took pleasure in calling to mind the modesty with which some of the sages had asked to have their dust scattered in a forest, in a field, or sprinkled in a fine, silvery rain into the course of a river. He imagined the lightness of ashes sown on the water, their swift course between shadowy banks; quickly they mingled with the water, became rushing water themselves long before disappearing into the sea or evaporating. Jean Calmet clearly saw this dead man's soul, serene in the clouds, assured of the fulfilment of his earthly destiny. He envied that dead man and that soul.

He tossed, turned; he strove to calm himself, repeating to himself that at this time his father's ashes were still at the crematorium in the padlocked, numbered aluminium box in which the mortician had placed them this very morning. When he finally had to fall asleep, he dreamt that he was clutching at black grass trying to reach the top of a hill. When he was halfway up, an enormous bull loomed suddenly against the night sky above him. The monster charged at him and crushed him. Later he often remembered this nightmare.

The Gymnase had granted him two days' leave for the ceremony. Today, Jean Calmet was still free. He began to think about the evening's gathering. It was set for eight o'clock in Lutry. They would gather around the dining-room table before the doctor's ghost at the head of the table. They would turn the pages of a catalogue: on the left-hand page, carefully reproduced in small black frames, there would be photos of the urns immediately available at the factory; on the right-hand page, their dimensions, their selling points, and a retail price sometimes corrected with a ballpoint pen. Jean Calmet was amazed at his new and deep interest in the most varied types of funeral equipment. A week earlier, he had known nothing about running a funeral notice in the papers or choosing a coffin, or about the calling cards of urn manufacturers and stonecutters. He had even been ignorant about the geography of the cemetery, despite the fact that he had driven along its interminable flank each time he had gone down to the edge of the lake. Early that morning, it seemed to him that an immense, subdivided domain had suddenly been thrown open to him, and that he rode around in it, marvelling at its diversity and hierarchies. Towards noon, as if he had not meant to, Jean Calmet walked down to the cemetery, admiring the number of mortuary establishments, sculptors, carvers, mosaicists whose workshops and storefronts were jammed together in the immediate vicinity. He had never noticed them before.

That morning, preoccupied by all that funereal variety, he forgot the real purpose of his visit. Then he remembered his father and grew gloomy. He entered the café where, yesterday morning at exactly the same time, tea had been served when they left the crematorium. This café bore a beautiful name: Le Reposoir. The waiters did not recognize him, but at the far end of the room – in a niche reserved for the doctor's family yesterday – another group was seated at the table in front of the same bottles, the same cups of tea, the same cakes; and this spectacle heartened Jean Calmet. Nothing mattered, since the same scenes could be enacted day after day without the owner or the waiters of the establishment noticing anything but a family in black, always the same, gathered three or four times a day at the back of the room to mark the passage of death.

Jean Calmet regained his self-control by an almost abnormal effort of will. As soon as his body felt the shadowy coolness of the café, his mind was enchanted by its solitude. Thank God, the doctor was nothing but a thin layer of ash at the bottom of a locked box. Branded on the box was a registry number which Jean Calmet had carefully entered in his notebook. This notebook was in his pocket. He felt for the slim pad through the corduroy of his jacket, over his heart, which was again beating regularly. Everything was all right.

Outside, the sun beat down on dazzling houses. With irritation, Jean Calmet thought of that evening's gathering. They were going to talk about the doctor again. The ghost of the enormous ruddy face would chortle at the head of the table. The five children would lower their voices to go into the details of the death and the inheritance. Their mother would cross the room without a word, she would disappear, she would return on tiptoe, a coffee pot in her hand; she would serve each of them in silence. The details of the death… Aghast, Jean Calmet realized that he knew nothing of his father's death. They had phoned the Gymnase to tell him the news; he had not received the call himself, and the sense of relief which he had felt like a delicious convalescence had prevented him from imagining his father's last moments at the time and had obliterated his curiosity later on, when he found himself in the company of the physician who had attended him up to the end. Then, it would have been an easy matter to find out (and even quite discreetly) about the way in which the doctor had met his end. But he hadn't questioned the physician. He had avoided his company. For just a moment, he had been next to him when they were entering the café, but the very fragmentary conversation had not gone beyond the banalities of the occasion. "It was terrible," repeated the mother, but that was the only word that fitted the Ogre, and, in any case, the commonplace vocable said nothing specific about the latest tragedy. It serves him right, thought Jean Calmet. I don't see why I should suffer while having them recount his end in detail. It was his turn to go, all right. There's some justice in the world. And he filled himself with this idea while savouring the regularity of his own pulse, which beat distinctly in his wrist, and the breath of air that inflated his lungs twelve times every sixty seconds. Air taken in and driven out. Throbbing of blood. If I played at choking, Jean Calmet said to himself, if I kept myself from breathing as in the past, everything would go black, I would see brownish circles whirling before my eyes, I would feel myself swelling, then bursting, I would hear the same church bells tolling wildly inside my skull… He was back on a plot of grass at the back of the garden in Lutry, he was seven years old, he was lying on the ground, and the stems of the new-mown grass pricked his shoulder blades through his thin shirt. All at once he had to die in order to be as valiant as the heroes and knights in the history books. He remembered Joan of Arc roasting in the flames, and Roland, mortally wounded, sounding the horn under the mountains, his lungs bursting into a shower of blood at the bottom of his throat. The little boy spread his arms like a condemned prisoner, took a huge gulp of air; suddenly he stopped his breath, and his martyrdom began: the brownish spots, the pinpoints burning like fireworks, the carillons in his ears… I'm suffering, Jean Calmet repeated to himself with pleasure, and something inundated his blood with a black fire that he would never forget. I have been chosen to suffer. I must resist fear, I must love this suffering. Vertigo seized him. A merry drunkenness of initiate and victim. Then he surrendered to panic, the air came back into him noisily, the sky regained its blue transparency where doves and gulls fled like trout.

Around that time, one of Jean Calmet's students had begun to grow thin and pale; green circles furrowed under her eyes.

Buboes grew under her arms, ganglions on her throat. There had been a first operation in September, and for a few weeks they thought she had been cured. Then the ganglions came back, and the girl's seat in Classics 2 was empty more and more frequently.

"Isabelle is going to die," Eugénie had said to Jean Calmet. "She knows it. We went over to her house with Alain to take pictures. Do you want to see them?"

It was at the end of a lesson one morning; the classroom was full of bright sunlight. Eugénie had pulled a packet of photos from a little orange knitted bag.

Isabelle.

The fiery black eyes, shining in deep sockets.

The emaciation of the face. Her pallor. Her dark hair, the bangs over her forehead, and, in that saint's face, appallingly alive, her large mouth, with the lower lip a little swollen, as for a last greedy beakful before the flight. Isabelle-who-is-going-to-die. And who knows it. And who fascinates her classmates.

Jean Calmet looked intensely at the condemned prisoner's face, the thin neck etched mysteriously by a single furrow which ran down into her checked blouse. Isabelle, her room, a close-up of her face. Jean Calmet's eye enters the girl's eye, wide-open at the bottom of a socket luminescent as silky plaster. Isabelle, her shoulders bare, her hand leaning against a Joan Baez poster, the four o'clock sun filtering through the near-closed blinds. Her face is closed, too, her eyes trained on the ceiling, her nose prim, her cheeks very gaunt, only her lip is swollen as if to kiss an invisible rakish lover. Isabelle, her teeth horribly white, in front of a bolted door. Isabelle cut in half, a single, black and fiery eye stares at Jean Calmet. Isabelle-who-is-going-to-die. And who knows it. And who – without knowing it – cuts into Jean Calmet's heart.

Isabelle came back to class only an hour or two each week, like a visitor, a woollen shawl over her shoulders, her pallor phosphorescent before the window. Then she was absent for a few weeks. Jean Calmet learnt from his students that she was growing thinner and thinner and that, once again, she had ganglions showing very plainly under her collarbones. Each day, after school, a little group of classmates went to see her in her small room in Sauvabelin; they tried to keep up a cheerful front but were terrified. She was not in bed. She sketched frenziedly, she wrote poems; fatigue seemed to have left her once and for all. Her parents did not disturb the teenagers: the father, a schoolmaster at the other Gymnase, smiled enigmatically in the hall. The mother brought them Coca-Cola and rolls, then disappeared at the back of the apartment.

Now Isabelle weighed no more than seventy-seven pounds. She came back again.

"I don't want to die a virgin," she told her friends.

She chose Marc, and they made love at the shore of the lake, hidden in the reeds, on a sleeping bag brought by Marc, one autumn night when the swans, the coots, the ducks answered one another on the misty water until dawn before the pink banks. Marc is handsome. He has a large nose, a lock of hair that crosses his brows. A boy of scarves and sweaters, who etches portraits of Isabelle on copper from which he makes prints for a few classmates, who sketches Isabelle in the nude before forests, who weaves purple and white tapestries. She chose Marc. She made love three or four times.

The necklace of ganglions showed on her neck horribly, an adornment of eternity. "We can't operate on them," the doctors said. She did not come to school at all any more.

When she weighed seventy-five pounds (that was two weeks before her death) she organized an outing to Crécy, a village on the Broye, hung on an amphitheatre of hills. Why Crécy? Her grandmother had a farm there. A small legacy. Childhood vacations. Harvest times. The cold spring at dawn after the first nocturnal stroll with a married soldier, just before her Communion, at fifteen and a half, he playfully threatens to splash you, all of a sudden he scoops up water in his hand, he pushes you back against the stone basin, smacks you with icy water and kisses you violently: his mouth – which still smells of wine and his cigar – thrusts a long tongue into your mouth, which takes away your breath and gathers your saliva right to the back of the antrum and the interstices of the teeth. You are fifteen and a half. Fresh young hair curling in your panties. Having your period for three years now – you are still not used to it. And your whole life ahead of you because you never dreamt that you would die at seventeen, the lord's angel, hypostasis of seventy-three pounds, now, little martyr tortured by the Auschwitz of God.

Isabelle was the one who led the expedition. They had their cameras. Marc was there, and Jacques, Eugénie, Anna, Alain and the Turk, Surène. They took the bus as far as Moudon, and from there they walked to Crécy, where they went straight to the cemetery without stopping at the café or the church, as Anna, who has a taste for the theatre, wanted them to marry Isabelle and Marc before the Lord's Table. The cemetery of Crécy lies a few hundred yards from the village, gently sloping over the immense valley. It was the time of year when the grass sprouts bright green, when the buds sparkle on the branches and the tepid wind melts the last patches of snow at the edge of the forests.

Isabelle knew that she had only two weeks to live.

At the end of the last lane, the last place before the fields, a pit is ready; the conical mound of earth waits to cover the coffin buried in the sweet, cold earth of Crécy.

The sun floods the cemetery.

Isabelle walks to her grave, stops for an instant at the edge of the hole, bends down and gathers in the palm of her hand a little of the earth that will cover her in two weeks.

The boys and girls are seated on two benches a few steps away; companions, brothers and sisters, quiet guardians obviously weakened by terror and tenderness. The dead girl now lies down in the bright sun on the grave next to her own. The gentle breeze goes through the cypresses, stirring them; a jay calls in the hedgerow, and from the valley rises the smell of brush fires on the far-off farmland hillsides.

Isabelle, they see her breathe, she is lying on the grave next to her own. She has crossed her hands over her breast, now she uncrosses them and, with her left hand, her arm outstretched, she touches, she caresses the sandy rim of her grave.

Anna has begun crying, she stands, she goes away by herself to the far end of the cemetery.

Alain and Jacques take pictures: Isabelle lying on her neighbour's flat tombstone, Isabelle feeling the edge of her grave, Isabelle walking to her grave barefoot, her wooden clogs under her arm, the wind lifting her dress over her thighs – perhaps it is a ghost going away down the long lane, the ghost's hair flies around her head, the jays talk to her about the beyond, where she must return – "Come back, adorable ghost of the most beautiful girl there ever was, return to the paths of lunar shadow where you were born, come back down into our ravines full of perfumed night!"

But Isabelle does not believe it. It is the stony soil that awaits her, and rotting, and melting in her planks that come asunder. Disgusting. God is a bastard. And Anna is still crying, her forehead crushed against the lichen-covered wall where strings of dark-pink lice run, the brothers of all the stillborn infants of the blissful valley.

Isabelle has moved on her flat slab, hiding her eyes from the terrible sun.

Silence. Then the jays. Crows, very far away, I'll never know them, they'll soar over this grave, they'll live two or three winters more than me, I'll be nothing but bones clad in a shred of cloth when they come plummeting down in their turn, little heaps of viscosities and frozen feathers, behind a November hedgerow. I don't want to think about my last dress. But I've already chosen the white one with the gold braid. The white one, the innocent one, my dress, O Marc, my Marc, since we've made love together. I won't die a virgin, Marc, my sweetheart, and you'll see me in my white dress, my hands clasped over the gold braids; Papa and Mama will seal the coffin, and you will come along with me to Crécy.

A bee has alighted on the tepid gravestone, Isabelle opens her eyes again, stretches out her arms alongside her body and touches the stone with her palms. Good sun, little bee already powdery with pollen. You have toiled in the first catkins of the hazel bushes, the primroses, the arnica, little bee, your honey will be warm this winter and I won't be here to taste it any more.

On this day, Isabelle weighs only seventy-seven pounds.

Through the cloth, the sun warms her round breasts, so well preserved, so fresh, so young on her impoverished ribs.

Now something tender is happening. Marc has got to his feet, he has gone up to the girl, he has seated himself beside her on the flat slab, he has placed his brown hand on Isabelle's pale forehead. He does not move, he says nothing, he sinks his gaze into the girl's intensely black eyes, he speaks to her with his gaze, he loves her, he stays on the border of day and night, he will remain in the light with the honey, the birds, the summer, she will go away, cold shadow, wandering shadow, into desolate space! O Marc. How noble your gesture was on that grave, that March afternoon, above the sunlit valleys. How gentle your hand was on the white brow, how your gaze was mysterious and clear in the gaze of that living girl who already speaks to you of the night.

Their eyes have filled with tears. They are crying, the children, they are crying noiselessly over their love, they are crying over their fearful loneliness. Who decides? Who condemns? Marc, Isabelle. She will live ten days, two weeks, they will put the white dress on her, the hearse will bring her from Lausanne to the cemetery that she wanted, to her little grave, to this sun.

Orpheus and Eurydice have lain down side by side on the slab, they listen to the wind in the grass, they breathe the smell of brush fire, shiver when they hear the jay's short, whistling call. The boys and girls have gone off to the far end of the cemetery, they watch the scene from afar, they will never forget it.

All of these things were told to Jean Calmet at the end of March, quite a long time afterwards, at the moment when the buds appeared on the branches, when the catkins covered themselves with yellow powder, when the bluish and pink pigeons made love on the turrets of the cathedral.

Always worried about being on time, Jean Calmet was the first to arrive at Les Peupliers, and he had to endure his mother's anxious conversation. He looked at the small grey woman with a pity full of hatred. He had come out of her. From her he got his slenderness, his frailty, his oversensitivity, and that all-too-famous intelligence which his father extolled in a loud voice, the better to make fun of him and humiliate him. Grey. Greyish. That was it, all right. His mother was some kind of startled and terrified old mouse.

She did not dare broach the one subject that interested him, she beat around the bush, fled. For the first time, Jean Calmet studied without fear the vast dining room where the polished brass gleamed in the rays of the setting sun. A bench ran along the wall, the big table was empty, but high-backed straw chairs marked each one's place. The head of the table, against the wall, was the father's territory. The doctor sat with his back a few inches from the solemn pendulum clock, a Morbier tall as a coffin, which came from the bottom of a Jura valley where a great-granduncle, guzzler of kirsch and psalms, had fiddled over it for a whole winter behind his little frost-covered windowpanes.

Jean Calmet looked at the clock. The copper of the dial stood out in the twilight. The slow, distinct tick-tock cut into the silence, and again Jean Calmet marvelled at the fact that his father had gone on sitting for years in front of this machine that stood like a monument behind him: as if he had wanted to associate himself symbolically with this power, as if he had wanted to warn all of them of his irrevocable domination. But his father was dead, and the tall Morbier went on hammering out its strokes in its case.

"You had today off too?" asked his mother, timidly.

Out of pity, Jean Calmet questioned her about the doctor. His mother brightened up. With a frightened pride in which he perceived everything that he hated about her – that pride of the tortured slave boasting of the master's harshness – she told him about his last days.

"He worked right up to the very end, you know, my poor Jean. Right up to the very end! Since his last attack, he's had trouble breathing, but he insisted on seeing all his patients every morning. He wouldn't let anybody down, and, in the afternoon, he never cut the visits short. He could have eliminated his house calls! But he wanted to see every one of his patients at home, without forgetting a single one. Not a single one. Right up to the end he cared for each and every one of them. He was a saint, my poor Jean. Can you imagine the effort that his sick heart must have had to make! He was choking, he had dizzy spells…"

With mounting anguish Jean Calmet recalled his excitement on those mornings when he had gone along with his father on house calls; he was eight, nine years old, they climbed interminable flights of stairs, they slammed doors of decrepit elevators; after the doctor had rung the doorbell twice, they would go into cluttered, airless apartments, into rooms thick with the sour smells of an unshaven, moaning old man.

Then came the hard, monotonous ballet: the sheets drawn back, the nightshirts raised up to the hips, the doctor palpating, driving a finger into a belly, pinching a roll of fat, stooping like a cannibal over a heart, grinding this flesh, flaccid and puffy, or dry, reddish, feverish, wounded, which succumbed to his formidable hands. Each time, genitals, buttocks spread apart, forests of hair. Moaning, hoarse breathing, dirty tears or tumours, pustules, spots, and all this wretchedness naked, all these exposed genitals, all these pubic regions like streaks of soot on deathly pale flesh made up a frightening, pallid gallery over which reigned the master of pain-racked, humiliated flesh. Seated in a corner and silent, or standing in the shadows, a little haggard, Jean Calmet stared wide-eyed at the scene, fascinated by the precision of his father's movements, sick with his strength and submitting, himself, to his sovereign rule. Sometimes the doctor needed him. He had to go back down to the courtyard, go after a bottle or a clean hypodermic needle in the trunk of the old Chevrolet, make tea in the kitchen for the sick person, dilute a powder in lukewarm water, carry it back to the bedside whose sourish odour brought a lump to his throat.

But, three days ago, the doctor's heart had burst. In his turn, the master had suffocated, throwing off the sheets, gesticulating like the ones he had treated, pushing away grotesquely the death that was tightening its grip on his chest. The tyrant had choked for hours, making a death rattle, rolling wild eyes, striking the air with his arms like a big baby; and, finally, the big red heart had exploded in its cage of ribs and meat.

Jean Calmet looked at his mother with new curiosity, wondering how she could have borne that guardianship for nearly fifty years. He was angry with her for her submissiveness. Everything could have been different – his life, Jean Calmet's own life would have been another life if she had rebelled. But for fifty years she had lived shrivelled up under the weight of the doctor's shouts, orders, furious caprices, voracious appetites and authoritarian manias. His father and mother both came from rather poor, rural families. They had married very young. He had worked like a madman to pay for his tuition – hodcarrier, ditch-digger, railway porter. At twenty-five years of age he had opened his surgery in Lutry and had stayed there. The wine-growers had adopted him: with them he drank hard, they were impressed by his strength. When the opportunity presented itself, he kissed their daughters, helped himself to the whorish waitresses of the cafés. He had a red face, an aquiline, shining nose, a large mouth. He reeked of cigars and white wine. He perspired... She was small, somewhat stooped. She kept in the background. They would find her stupefied and motionless for a moment, not daring to enter the room where the doctor was reading his newspaper, belching curses aimed at the world as a whole. Or the craned neck, listening, more of a mouse, more of a shrew than ever, for the heavy footfalls crunching in the gravel of the terrace and the slam of the car door: a moment of peace. But the master came back soon, exploded, turned everything upside down, and the trotting from one room to another recommenced, the quick, uneasy running, the hesitation, the long waits before the doors where her children surprised her, embarrassed, wounded by her terrors, and too sure of their own fear to dare push her to audacity.

The mortuary representative arrived at the same time as his brothers and sisters. Everyone sat around the table. Ceremonious, dressed in black, the man took a long brochure from his briefcase and opened it, deliberately, on the table.

"First of all, I'd like to offer our firm's condolences," he said in a gentle voice. "We know that stricken families need our services. And we make every effort to give them complete satisfaction. For Monsieur your father, he was cremated yesterday, and, I believe, you want to order an urn..."

Everyone fell silent. The mortuary representative paused, to make the importance of his message felt, then he resumed with impressive eloquence:

"Naturally, our firm offers twenty different models – from the most expensive, the most sophisticated to the most modest item. Exactly the same for the caskets. The whole range, from massive oak upholstered with silk, to the plain pine box rented for the occasion. But that's beside the point. Let's look at the urns."

He coughed slightly and held his catalogue open so that everyone seated around the table could see distinctly the sketches and photos that shone with electric colours on the slick, gleaming paper. His colourless face beamed with gravity against his dark mortuary salesman's suit. Carrion-eater, thought Jean Calmet, you make money from a dirty trade, you fatten up your bosses with an odd kind of ash. Then he realized that he envied the self-confidence of the pale, serene man with the face of a bold ibis who, several times a day and perhaps each evening, helped to solve the problems of families that bereavement had just ensnared in inextricable obligations. The man paraded the catalogue under the eyes of the onlookers.

"You see, Mesdames and Messieurs, that we have all kinds of urns." (He was very pleased with himself.) "Type A1," he resumed, "the most expensive, is made of white Carrara marble. The item is heavy: twenty-seven pounds, twenty-four inches high. A very stable model. Obviously, it isn't cheap, but you won't find a more beautiful one on the market. Look at those curves, those brilliant reflections. A work of art!"

And he stuck his index finger respectfully under the photo of a large vase that looked as if it had been carved out of a block of snowy, intolerably pure ice.

"Type A2," he continued after striking an admiring pose, "is also very fine work. It's made of pink cherry with red and brown spots, with mouldings, round foot, matching lid, warranty of origin, twenty-four pounds, twenty-two inches. Your cat or dog can play around it and there's no chance of his knocking over a piece like that. Model B1 is also made of marble, a genuine clouded marble. Look at the little encrusted shells, they're specially imported for our firm. This article comes in two sizes. On request, we'll supply you with the large size, which can hold the ashes of two persons. It's practical, by the way: lots of people find it reassuring to know that someday their ashes will be mixed with the ashes of the deceased."

Jean Calmet gave a sudden start. Around the table, nobody had moved. The solemn bird turned the page:

"Model B2 is a very handsome imitation marble, green or black, inscription in gold at the firm's expense. Model C is a handcrafted bronze. Sides trimmed with embossed designs, choice of tulip corollas or ivy leaves. Type D is made of steel, with studded handles, and a little lid fitted with a key gives you the same security as a strongbox. Let me point out, by the way, that this model also comes in miniature, the size of a pigeon egg, for the ashes of stillborn babies: the item can be slipped easily into your luggage, into a suitcase, for example, into a lady's handbag, so you can take your little dear departed on trips. Naturally, for the big urns, the adult urns, it's more difficult. But all our merchandise is supplied with base, on request. We do the installing ourselves in your parlour, in your living room, in your office, to suit your requirements. That way, you aren't separated from your dear departed."

For the second time, Jean Calmet shuddered violently. At all costs he must avoid having his father's urn remain at Les Peupliers. It had to be locked up far from here, imprisoned behind a solid iron gate, one that was permanent. He took the floor in an anxious voice:

"Isn't there some way of leaving the urn at the columbarium? Surely there are vacant pigeonholes? That way, our friends could pay their last respects to our father without invading this house…"

"Nothing simpler," replied the salesman, to Jean Calmet's great relief. "A simple phone call and we straighten the affair out with the crematorium. We make no charge at all. Later on, we submit a bill, it all goes like clockwork. You can also acquire a grant for twenty-five years. At the end of the twenty-fourth year, you're notified of the expiration by the proper authorities – in this case, the Bureau of Burials and Cinerary Monuments, down at the Town Hall, and you've got plenty of time to make your arrangements. Besides, there are periodic reminders printed in the newspapers."

He added, as if for himself:

"Yes, that's a good way to handle it, the columbarium. And then you've got the caretaker who keeps the pigeon-holes spic and span, he dusts them every morning, your urn shines like a new penny!"

Jean Calmet imagined the caretaker in a blue smock, a cotton mop in his hand, carefully dusting each piece of marble or brass, persisting, searching the nooks behind the sinister vase, hunting down the dust on the partitions of the box and on the handles, on the indentations, on the grooves of the lid, on the raised design of the belly of the urn, with the meticulousness of a maniac supervised by an assembly of shadowy ghosts. But there was one word that troubled him more than anything: it was *pigeonhole*, which immediately stirred up visions of watered-silk flights, coo-ings, swellings of grey and pale-pink feathers, amorous little conversations – all of which "columbarium", another word suggesting the caress of wings and tepid feathery embraces, had already begun to evoke after the mortician's salesman had uttered it in complete innocence. Thus, that place of refuge in its enclosing wall of cypresses acquired a subtle grace, the lightness of a precious birdcage where the sun, filtered in regular rays by the black trees, cast rainbow col-ours on wing quills, lit up a beak, set ablaze coral eyelids, pink-pearl feet, interminable demonstrations of tenderness at the back of cool cubicles.

The salesman gone, they passed the catalogue around the table for a long time. Jean Calmet looked at his broth-ers and sisters in amazement. Never had he felt so distant from them. Having been forced to remain silent during the fellow's explanations, they were now excited and spoke all the louder. His gaze went from one to the other with amenity. Étienne, the agricultural engineer, tall, ruddy like his father, but not so strong, less powerful; he had married too soon in order to escape the doctor. Then Simon, the teacher, tawny and slender – Simon, who had been in trouble because he had locked himself up with some boys all summer in a mountain chalet. Simon, the mother's favourite. Simon who had spent his childhood curled up in her, taking refuge in her skirts, in her secrets, in her plaintive whisperings. Simon, the ornithologist. Simon who ran through the woods, with a pair of field glasses screwed to his eyes, Simon whom Jean Calmet envied because he always had a young man lying beside him on lookout, or kneeling at his side, to put bands on the foot of a jay, to caress with a gentle finger the silken head of a titmouse caught in the net they had stretched between two apple trees in the garden. He did not like his two brothers. But, still, he understood, he fathomed those two, the eldest and the younger one. From his sisters, on the contrary, emanated an opaque mystery, which had constantly alienated him from them and had created in him a fear mingled with anguish and remorse. Hélène, blonde, robust, the nurse who spoke with the doctor for hours about operations, shock treatments, and all the nasty tittle-tattle of the hospital. And Anne, who was two years older than he was, Anne, who did nothing, who travelled; they got postcards from Sweden, from the United States, she would disappear, come back engaged, she became engaged again and learnt a new language, a new country, before burying herself in other complications on her return.

Jean Calmet was the youngest, the "*benjamin*", the little Benjamin, as they had told him thousands of times throughout his childhood, to the point that this word became detestable to him, so that he would blush with shame and anger, in Sunday School and at catechism, when the pastor told the story of Jacob's last son: "Rachel died in labour, she had wished to name her son Ben-oni, son of my sorrow, but her father called him Benjamin, which means son of my right hand..." And he, Jean Calmet, bore the middle name Benjamin, which was written on his official papers, which explained the repulsion he felt on showing his passport, his identity card, his military-service booklet or any other document reminding him of this hated name.

He would repeat it to himself when he was alone, to make himself suffer, feeling the weight of its consonants: Jean-Benjamin Calmet, he persisted. Jean-Benjamin Calmet, Les Peupliers, Lutry, Vaud. Jean-Benjamin Calmet, student of literature. Rifleman Jean-Benjamin Calmet, Company VII, section 4, in the field. Jean-Benjamin Calmet, teacher at the Gymnase Cantonal de la Cité, No. 78, Chemin de Rovéréaz, Lausanne.

The children of Doctor Paul Calmet and Madame Calmet, née Jeanne Rossier. A family. A lineage. Come my sons, run my daughters, you shall warm my limbs, your strength shall soothe the days of my old age, and when I am no more, you will care for my ashes. In this way you will know that I am not completely dead, since my race lives on in you until the end of generations. Étienne, Simon, Hélène, Anne and Jean. The end of generations... Jean Calmet restrained himself from smiling ironically: Étienne alone had children and the doctor did not want to know them – far from it, his nephews having struck him as dishevelled, screaming savages on the rare occasions when he had come upon them unexpectedly at Les Peupliers.

Jean Calmet looked pensively at the faces of his brothers and sisters under the lamp. So his father's death had changed nothing? They had the same tense expressions, the same irritating and almost fearful gestures as they passed around the catalogue. His brothers were still trying to take themselves seriously. They played their orphans' role with a diligence that was painful. Hélène and Anne were still those strangers who attracted and repelled with their wrinkles full of sticky moistness. No, nothing had changed; just as before, the ticking of the clock haunted the room interminably, the lamp had the same orange colour, tinting the brass work and the dark bench; he saw the lake through the open window, the night was blue against the black water, and all the way at the back of the landscape, under the mountains, shone the little lights of Évian. Just as before. Nothing had changed. Sadness invaded Jean Calmet's flesh, burdening it like an intolerable weariness. He busied himself looking at the catalogue to escape himself; he shook himself, suddenly he exulted inwardly. The father was dead and they had burned him at the crematorium. The doctor, dead. A little heap of ashes! Aloud, commenting on them, he read over the description of the articles most recommended by the salesman, describing in detail certain points, reconsidering others, he spoke offhand in a clear, loud voice, as if he had analysed a text before his students.

They agreed on the brocaded urn. Type B1. Everyone admired this shelly marble, the grey-brown of the stone tended slightly towards gold, its delicacy and name reminded them of velvet. The item had a very natural look because of the fossilized shells that brightened up the marble: everyone thought that it suited the father's *elementary* tastes. They chose the single-place model. Étienne was assigned the task of placing the order with the Mortuary.

On his way home, Jean Calmet came across a porcupine and looked at it for a long time. He had left his car in the garage; he was climbing back up the Chemin de Rovéréaz with short steps, when he noticed a scraping in a hedge, then a breath, a sort of melodious, repetitive moan that stifled itself in grunts. It may seem strange to relate this encounter with a porcupine so absent-minded that he did not even notice Jean Calmet. For several days, this meeting was to have a benevolent meaning for him: as an auspicious omen given to him by the animal; a lesson in savagery on the edge of the damp gardens under the half-moon in the blue grass.

First of all, Jean Calmet saw very beautiful eyes shining under the lower branches of a laurel tree: a dark pupil ringed with gold around which long hair, also gold, watered silk, made a gaudy patch. The nose moved, greedy, wet, a little black cherry at the end of a snout with very smooth, ebony hair. Motionless, amazed, Jean Calmet wondered if the animal was going to catch sight of him and vanish. Something in him wished, almost irrationally, that it would stay. The animal had advice to give him. All of Jean Calmet's senses reached out towards it – towards that neat, solid head which stood out, clearly lit by the moon, against its background of black leaves. There was a squealing in that shadow and the body appeared, long and lithe, borne by a belly round with strange sensuality. The short little legs ran a few inches, the nose scented the ground, the belly undulated, round and full, under the armour bristling with quills whose white points made a silvery halo that lightened, made spiritual, this prodigiously terrestrial apparition.

Jean Calmet listened to the warning rise in his flesh, throwing him into confusion. Perfectly motionless, he suddenly felt riddled with the odours of sunken roads, wet grass, rotting humus, trails made by slugs, feather-legged insects, wily, fearful rodents, as if drops of vigour had shot into him violently from the depths of the secret ground, intoxicating him, jolting him, filling him with fresh, new excitement. The animal's wildness was extraordinary among the carefully tended gardens, the sumptuous villas. Emerging from the earth intact and powerful, the pure animal, marvellously innocent under his crown of silver thorns, was the primitive sign that Jean Calmet had always been waiting for, the symbol of a wild, happy freedom, proof that no domination ever subjugates the great telluric forces that well up, that spurt, that run in the midst of the aberrations of buildings.

The porcupine was silhouetted against the road with the precision of a heraldic figure. The moon turned the asphalt white. From silver stone to the squatting porcupine outlined with sand, Jean Calmet thought curiously, beginning to catch his breath. A long minute went by, during which the wind stirred the leaves of the hedges, the odour of the ground became denser, almost aggressive, so heavily was it loaded with emanations that were putrescent and, at the same time, brand new like the milky savour of roots. The porcupine remained standing there, black and phosphorescent with quills. All of a sudden, it started on its way again, it finished crossing the road, insinuated itself into the grass and vanished under a hazel bush. Jean Calmet could still hear it stirring, its needles squeaking against the bark of trees; an insect cracked in the animal's snout, and then only the wind going through the leaves could be heard. The shadows closed up again. The animal had returned to its mystery.

In the months that followed, Jean Calmet was to encounter a few other augural animals. On that particular night, he fell asleep without effort and slept deeply. On waking the next morning, he did not remember having had any bad dreams. No bull, no father coming down a hill and crushing him. He saw this as a favourable sign and was glad to be back at the Gymnase.

Jean Calmet closes the door of the teachers' room and starts down the already deserted corridor where the bust of Ramuz, black, sinister, shoots a vacant gaze at the little sink belonging to the secretary's office. Jean Calmet walks slowly, as if some sly mechanism has just gone awry within him. Nevertheless, the morning has gone well, he has given his lessons with the gladness of new starts… He is struck dumb on the square. The bells of the cathedral are striking twelve noon. Great solemn booming at the top of the hill, bronze bouncing over the whole countryside around, celestial orchestra of the monks and bishops supplanted by Calvinists in square caps. An oblique magpie flees before trembling poplars like powdered halos. Jean Calmet stops, his legs give way beneath him, but his gaze photographs the gay scene: the little trees, the sandstone of the edifice all yellow in the sun, and the misty precipice dropping to the town square, under the hill. There is something of a tang in the air after the bells, something almost funny, mocking him… Jean Calmet begins walking again, convinced that he is the only anxious soul in that honey-coloured light. He has given good lessons: Petronius, Apuleius. His students like to read with him. The writers of the decline seem open, accomplices. They despise Cicero and Virgil, who strike them as lackeys of power and whom they associate with school boredom, compositions, marks on translations. On the contrary, the magic of the times of strife, their oriental connections, their kind of irrational passion, attract them, fascinate them, and each class, in its turn, finds itself excited by the witches, werewolves and roguery of Apuleius. But this weariness, this fear in his limbs? Jean Calmet heads towards the Café de l'Évêché. A group of girls in blue jeans overtakes him, they laugh, they speak in loud voices, their long hair hangs over their still-tanned shoulders. Jean Calmet goes into the Café de l'Évêché and sits down at the only free table before the front window. He orders a Ricard and becomes engrossed, gloomily, in contemplating the scenery. Just then, the beautiful kids in jeans go by on the right bank of the Bessières bridge, they act like fools, pushing one another, turning around, their gesticulation stands out like a challenge against the grey-blue sky. Jean Calmet feels them – marvellously gay and strong – and he receives, right in his heart, the familiar blow.

He takes a sip of Ricard.

Bad for worriers, Ricard. It hits the nerves too fast. Two opaque wings on each side of the brain, the sweetish taste that burns, that heaves the stomach into the gullet: he is far from being in the resounding health of the Gymnase students. Jean Calmet sinks into his malaise as if it were a woolly reverie. Why has he become a teacher? To escape adults? He knows all too well that the most terrible adult has always been his father, even in death. The classrooms that he has entered and that he will henceforth enter are refuges from the authority of that father who is bearing down with all his weight on the rest of the world. Precarious refuge, threatened all the more by the fact that the dead man's spirit enters it more readily than his huge carcass! For what reason, at this particular moment, is Jean Calmet thinking about the chalet at one summer's end in his childhood with an almost desperate nostalgia? Because he is lonely and weary? He recalls the scenery perfectly: in the evening, the wind comes from the bottom of the valley and puts to flight the leaves of the plane trees; they do not fly away like the leaves of the other trees, they flee horizontally towards the fabulous mountains in the shadows already full of bells. Down below lies the dried-up valley. There, it is the whirling coolness that carries off the leaves into the violent indigo of the sky... Jean Calmet recalls his father and mother seated under the red lamp of the panelled room; he alone is with them, he is reading *Treasure Island*, he stands up, he goes near the window and the wind blows his locks down into his eyes. The scene settles before him with sharp clarity: the grass buffeted against the chalet, the purple night, inside the lamp, his father's white shirt open on his greying hair, his mother slightly withdrawn from the light, a magazine on her lap; they fall silent for a long time, they listen to the moan of the foehn in the plane trees. Ah, everything was possible then, says Jean Calmet to himself when the happy picture is torn: he used to carve boats out of pine, he could read pirate stories, decorate the block of butter with the tine of a fork, imagine ghosts running in the attic, try to catch up with the doctor on the scree or tirelessly follow the flight of jackdaws on the white ridge, like an embroidery with raucous cries whose threats make you smile.

At a single gulp, Jean Calmet drains his Ricard and his eyes turn back to the old picture: he was protected in those days, cared for; life was before him, open, possible, nothing would destroy certainty and tenderness...

He is shaken by a shudder. Around him, working men in blue overalls, shopkeepers in white smocks pay their bills before going back to their garages and shops. The first Gymnase students of the afternoon begin to replace them in small, laughing flocks; they sit down and light cigarettes, order coffee, the boys put their arms around the girls' necks. Jean Calmet cannot manage to get to his feet and leave. No determination. The morning's strength is gone. But as if it were the revenge of the Gymnase, pure place, on the world of adults and serious people, it pleases him that the Café de l'Évêché is periodically invaded by the young people who restore their own order. Or their disorder! But nobody can read his thoughts since the doctor died; this idea also cheers him. With satisfaction, he touches the band of black silk that has crossed his lapel for six days. Some of his students give him a kindly greeting. He orders cold meat to keep up a brave face and forces himself to eat it all. Two-fifteen is drawing near, the hour of classes: the groups call to one another, get to their feet; in the street there is a colourful uproar, an elbowing of big children with long hair, a parade of necklaces made of tiny bells, saris, faded blue jeans, anti-nuclear bomb insignia, US Army field jackets, curly beards and gleaming teeth. Then nothing more. The bell in the cathedral strikes the quarter-hour. In the deserted café, the waitress empties the ashtrays into a big aluminium can that she takes from one table to the other, grumbling. Jean Calmet rises, goes out, starts up the Rue de la Mercerie with little, dreamy steps.

He pushed the door of the little shop and was happily surprised by the rather vulgar cosmetic odour that reigned. For the half-hour to be absolutely complete and good, that strongly sweetish odour was necessary. He was also happy to be the only customer in the barber's shop at that hour: Monsieur Liechti would have plenty of time, would spoil him, would coddle him. Jean Calmet was going to be able to give himself up to his pleasure without witness. Another prerequisite: no impatient gaze in his back. No newspaper nervously rustled or shaken, no warning cough, no throat-clearing over his shoulders... Seated on a wicker armchair in the middle of his little shop, Monsieur Liechti was reading an Italian magazine. He brightened up, rose, and Jean Calmet experienced a comforting sense of tranquillity at seeing once more the long, wide-set teeth, the sunken cheeks and the high, bald forehead of the old barber. A whitish comb emerged from the little pocket of his blue smock. With a theatrical movement, he invited Jean Calmet to be seated in one of the two worn leather chairs. Jean Calmet sat down, tipped himself backwards slightly, his neck met the coolness of the headrest. He was immediately overwhelmed by a pleasure that announced the coming of more complete happiness. But there could be no haste. Monsieur Liechti's movements were slow, meticulous, and Jean Calmet was enchanted by those preliminaries in the silent shop where the sharp emanations of the eau de cologne floated.

It was not by chance that Jean Calmet had become accustomed to abandoning himself on these premises. Old-fashioned, foreign, the shop had few customers. What is more, an unceasingly valuable advantage for the person who wants to sink uninterruptedly into himself, Monsieur Liechti was not one of these barbers who bore their victim with sports chitchat. He was silent, and only one brief question: "No haircut today? Just a shave?" came legitimately from his thin mouth.

He tied a towel around the neck of Jean Calmet, who once again marvelled at the transformation that this simple piece of cloth immediately brought about in his face. In the mirror, which was somewhat moth-eaten at the corner where it joined the shelf of artificial marble, his features were curiously sunken, prominent. Their clarity was striking against the immaculate sheet, and Jean Calmet looked at himself, for once, without severity and without ill temper.

Monsieur Liechti took a glass box from a shelf and shook it over an aluminium bowl which began to fill with a slightly granular flour. He added tepid water, and, with little strokes of the shaving brush, he raised in the receptacle a lather that sparkled over the wood panelling of his shop. For several minutes, the shaving brush turned round and round in the thickening foam. Then Monsieur Liechti raised the instrument into the light and gauged the consistency of the cream with satisfaction. Only then did he begin to apply it to Jean Calmet's face, in wide, flat bands whose order he soon disturbed with a stiff brush, soaping for a long time the face of his customer, who closed his eyes, his head thrown back under its strong, steady pressure. The lathering filled Jean Calmet with a calm and coolness that sent shivers down to his knees.

Now Monsieur Liechti took hold of his razor and honed the long blade on the leather, broad as an army belt, which he pulled and stretched with his left hand. It was a knife of steel, gleaming, with a yellow horn handle, whose blade made a quick, regular whispering on the strop.

Then, with a thumb, he tested the edge:

"Let's get to work, Monsieur Calmet!" he said, smiling with his wide-set teeth. And with his left hand, taking up the shaving brush, he revivified the suppleness of the cream on the cheeks and chin.

The razor began to run over the patient's skin with prodigious delicacy. First, around the sideburns, the line of which he marked accurately, then along the cheeks, respecting the symmetry with exact movements: razor stroke to the left, squeaking slide, immediately followed by a pass on the right cheek, return to the left and extension of the operation to the outlines of the lips; the razor immediately moved to the other side, the mouth twisted a little to stretch the skin, which in this way gave itself up flatter and more readily to the keen blade. As if he wished to leave nothing to chance, Monsieur Liechti came back once more to the summit of the cheeks and ran the blade carefully, but without pressing, over the clear zone.

His eyes closed, Jean Calmet experienced new bliss. He felt deep, light peace; each caress of the razor was a delicate attention that overwhelmed him. He no longer remembered his solitude or weariness. He abandoned himself to those hard, adept fingers, to that dry blade, to the acidulated odour of the smock and the shop, to the regular little sound of the razor, the gentle scraping, hissing, sliding which lulled him, benumbed his memories, roused on the surface of his whole skin a delight that spread out. Now Monsieur Liechti firmly tilted the head back and attacked the chin with tiny circular touches: the blade moved with greater circumspection, turned, came back flat under the lip, tarried again, while the barber's index finger and thumb pinched the skin over and over, held it back, fashioned

44

it over to suit the razor which unceasingly increased and improved its effect.

Then the edge went down along the Adam's apple and followed the collar of the towel, it climbed back up the throat with short strokes, the left slope, the right slope, reached the ear, came back down, dallied in a small, untouched zone, ran anew up to the sideburns, returned to the nostrils, scratched, gnawed with its rounded point, polished the cheeks, sanded the chin.

Peaceful bliss haunted Jean Calmet.

Monsieur Liechti set his razor on the shelf of fake marble.

He added a little lukewarm water to the lather, rotated the shaving brush in the bowl, coated Jean Calmet's cheeks and neck once more, took up the razor, honed the blade anew and, very slowly, as if to remove the foam from the skin, ran through all his strokes again: the face seemed smooth, and gleamed slightly in the mirror.

Monsieur Liechti raised a section of the towel, placed a warm sponge there, touched Jean Calmet behind the ears and under the jaw. He immediately unstoppered a large frosted-glass bottle and splashed all of his skin with stinging eau de cologne, tart as a sourball; his whole face suddenly burned and quickly grew cold almost as soon as the alcohol evaporated. Monsieur Liechti shook the towel, fanned Jean Calmet; a shudder went over his whole body.

"Now for the comb!"

Monsieur Liechti combed Jean Calmet's hair carefully.

It was finished.

Jean Calmet paid, shook Monsieur Liechti's extended hand, paused for an instant on the doorstep of the shop. The air was good, the light golden, September was nearing its end, the afternoon sun was turning the old street russet... Jean Calmet drew in a deep breath and went on his way, dawdling around the windows of small shops. He thought of the pleasure that he had just known, he was still relaxed, borne by a special joy: it was in his fibre like a force that tried to make itself known, make itself loved, new power. Jean Calmet also looked at the passers-by with new confidence, studying their faces and clothes, examining their bearing, admiring the women most of all, scrutinizing their eyes, marvelling at the diversity of their appeal and at the gleam smouldering at the bottom of their pupils. Several of them gave him back a look that burned Jean Calmet right to the depths of his skull. So could he be happy, too? He could count for something, be noticed, be stared at in the crowd by a woman. People were interested in him, people recognized him. It seemed to him that one wench peeked at him, feigning innocence, that salesgirls crossed his eye through shop windows and did not turn away immediately. Jean Calmet stopped, he greedily studied their hair, their skin, their movements, he guessed their desires and disillusion, he sniffed at trails, he made up rendezvous and affairs, he imagined intelligent, voluptuous liaisons, a whole autumn of uninterrupted tenderness and trust.

He did not hurry. His lessons for the next day were prepared; thinking about them gave him another reason to rejoice. In honour of the *Metamorphoses*, he dubbed twin sisters Photis and Psyche; blonde and tanned, the girls were stepping out of a pop fashion boutique laden down with huge multicoloured plastic bags. He ate a hot dog in the open air and drank a mug of beer at the Café du Pont, from where he became engrossed in watching the throngs at the doors of the department stores.

The street lights went on.

The mildness of September made a kind of halo around people and things that the street lamps illuminated in the pink light of evening.

It was when he came back to the little Place de la Palud that he staggered, thought he was fainting, had to lean against a wall to keep from falling: his father was walking placidly on the other side of the square. His father! Covered with sweat, Jean Calmet dug his nails into the sandstone of the Hôtel de Ville. His eyes popping, he stared at the ghost in desperation: it was the doctor all right, there could be no doubt about it, the heavy footfalls peacefully taking possession of the pavement, the breadth of the shoulders, the profile red and satirical under the tilted hat. The apparition stopped before a café, one hand extended towards the doorknob... Terrified, Jean Calmet ran his fingers over his dripping brow. He was not thinking, he trembled, he was breathing wildly; and, on the other side of the square, twenty yards away, that horrible slow-motion film: his father pushing the café door, the big horrifying silhouette going inside, the door closing behind it.

Consciousness came back to him with a feeling of bitter cold that chilled him from head to foot. A truck with a trailer went by, hiding from him the café where the ghost was now drinking his white wine, a cigar in his hand, his hat lying on the table before him. Jean Calmet made up his mind suddenly, ran across the square, plunged into the Café du Raisin: no doctor. Four or five solitary customers were sipping their drinks, and, at the back of the room, under the clock, a big fellow, vaguely ruddy, round-shouldered, his eyes shot with fatigue... Was this the man that he had taken for his father? Unthinkable... barely a minute or two ago, the doctor had gone by slowly on the cobbled pavement; Jean Calmet had recognized his profile perfectly, his lumbering stride; the doctor had his hat at a rakish angle, his trousers full of twisted wrinkles, his thick, hard strength seeming to radiate... Jean Calmet went home. Now a sharp pity replaced his fear: his father was dead and he came back among the living like a wanderer because he was unhappy, restless, perhaps desperate. Who would help him? What aid was he calling for from the beyond? Disgust gripped Jean Calmet's stomach. Then he would never be at peace. No respite. The autumn dampness fell on his shoulders. He shut himself up in his lair, shivering, and stuffed himself with sleeping pills to be certain of getting some rest.

The disgust lasted into the next day. His classes over, Jean went back home and began answering the pile of condolence letters which had been cooling off on his table for a week. "…Profoundly touched by your solicitude… moved by your sympathy…" – he lined up the formulas, distracted from his writing by the faces of his correspondents, colleagues, former students, classmates from the University: between his letter and him, a whole gallery of ironic judges who saw through the emptiness of his clichés as he used them over and over. More insidiously, fear and doubt had crept into him in the afternoon and had not ceased to grow since he had opened the black-bordered envelopes, read the funereal notes, begun himself to write his replies. He thanked people for having written to him on his father's death. But yesterday, at the Place de la Palud, the ghost… Was the doctor really dead? All morning Jean Calmet berated himself for his ridiculous visions. He had allowed himself to fall into the trap all afternoon, the trap of the deceptive sweetness of life; and to punish him, there had been the apparition, that ghost, that grotesque hallucination. On his tongue, the bitter taste of the sleeping pills, and remorse in his heart, reprobation that would not be stilled the whole morning; he swore to himself that he would not again be taken in by that phantasm. The doctor roaming around the city! He had to be overemotional and weak to allow himself to be taken in by the first vague resemblance that came along unexpectedly. He could not find enough words to reproach himself, to belabour himself. That evening, things were simpler, uneasiness stole over him. "…Since your father died, my dear Jean…" He pushed away the last note with anger and, from his briefcase, took a treatise on public health which he had borrowed from the library of the Gymnase that very afternoon, making sure that no one had seen him.

He opened it to page 215 and read with the utmost attention the article that he had hastily glanced at in the bays lined with books. It was entitled 'The Signs of Death', and Jean Calmet studied it word for word:

Aside from the cessation of respiration, the signs of death are the following:

1. Cessation of heartbeat.
2. Absence of pupillary and corneal reflexes; the darkening of the eyes.
3. Drop in body temperature: below 20° centigrade, death is certain.
4. Onset of bodily rigidity.
5. Onset of bodily spots: bluish-red spots on the lower parts.
6. Bodily decomposition.

Immediately, Jean Calmet was ashamed of having borrowed that stupid book. His childishness oppressed him like a physical defect: he saw himself again at the library, uneasy, furtive, nervously slipping the book into his open briefcase... His father had died on 17 September. They had burned him at the crematorium on the twentieth. In the intervening time, and since the first moments that followed the death, Dr Gross had had to sign the certificate after determining death. Proper death. Undeniable death, from which no one ever returns. Jean Calmet began to muse over the red and blue spots of corpses. The lower parts. The big white thighs mottled with red streaks like imitation marble. It grieved Jean Calmet to think vulgarly of Gorgonzola, soft cheese; it, too, was stained bluish, with verdigrised dough like dead veins in rigid flesh. Dirty specks at the calf of the leg and on the knees. Wounds, purplish-blue ocelli, sanguine bruises. On the knees! Jean Calmet remembered a detail that was commonly related about crematoria: the kneecaps withstood fire. The attendant had to remove them from the ashes with a small shovel; then he threw them into a burlap bag that soon resembled a bag of marbles, clicking funereally. Childish vision! But, for a moment, this legend amused Jean Calmet, distracting him from the anguish that had gripped him for hours. His mind wandered around the torture rack of St Lawrence, the flames of the Inquisition, the ovens of Auschwitz. Good deal, thought Jean Calmet. Really the final solution. Take a heretic, beat him, lock him up, fine him, banish him, catch him again, beat him once more, resolutely he refuses to keep still, he stubbornly persists, he speaks again! Burn him. That's silence. You remove him shape and all. Fire! The beautiful purifier! Your man is no more than a few ashes to be thrown in the river or to be abandoned to the wind. And he had never heard ashes speak! Jean Calmet thought with contentment, grasping at once the whole scope of his error. It's just the opposite! he flung at himself in a hard, ironic tone. The cruder the torture, the more the ashes speak. The remains of the persecuted are not reduced to silence. The crosses of the Inquisition, the fires of St John's Eve, the piles of shoes, the heaps of gold teeth at Auschwitz proclaim victory. Ashes are alive, loquacious, vindictive; they are reincarnated, they return to the charge, they teach, they triumph, they persecute in their turn! The saint's torture grill has more power than the tools of his executioners. Those who die by the flame come back and speak. And the bodies destroyed in the fire... The vision of his father in the oven of the crematorium of Montoie shocked Jean Calmet. The doctor's flesh had cracked in the fearsome heat, fissures had yawned, belching fat, spitting water, holes were gaping, bounded by bloated edges, the sweat had smoked in the faults, the whole tortured body came asunder, collapsing, and, in the end, it had melted at the bottom of the oven, a horrid, gluey incandescence that dwindled, flattened out, then had cooled slowly, a greyish mass of bone and viscera, then cinders, meagre sand, a thin layer of dust tamped down in the obscurity of the oven, whose heating units also grow cold and contract, buzzing… Sadness gripped him. A weariness born of remorse and horror compressed his thorax. He had trouble remaining seated at his table, overloaded with books and students' homework papers; it was as if some violent blow had broken his spine at the level of the collarbones, and the pain gripped his trunk, crushed his lungs, made his heart leaden. His lamp cast a double light, white at the bottom, red on top, over the walls lined with books and etchings of his study. His study! One more term that he had acquired in Lutry just as one might catch a disease. "Papa is in his study. Papa is calling you in his study. Hurry! Jean, what are you standing there for? Papa wants to see you in his study!" He had to drop everything, run, go rushing down the echoing steps, push open the door of the den where the red doctor gleamed in the light of his lamp, behind his file cards and folders, while the shadow of his gestures moved, enormous, on the bookcase. And his voice. At once an aggressive tone, perhaps because the doctor was too rushed by his work to soften, to explain, to listen to others who submitted to him at once. Jean Calmet remembered his humiliation: he was standing before his father, just waiting for the moment when he might flee, but he had to listen to orders, submit to the torrent, the laughter, the rage, the joking, all that concentrated strength that burst like a storm on his head. Overbearing tone. The eyes that burn your heart. The wounding words rained down:

"Little moron, imbecile, you'll never amount to anything. When I think that I'm killing myself for all of you – for you in particular, for your schooling, for your pleasure – and what reward do I have? A cringing, muddle-headed weakling who goes around sulking all day long. If at least you worked hard at school! But nothing at all. Nothing doing. Monsieur puts off his exams, plays truant from his seminars and spends most of his time in the cafés of La Cité. Drinking wine. And with whom, if I may ask? With little buggers like himself, ship's lawyers, parasites, flops, chatterboxes. Nice company, my friend. Your books? Your classes? Your fine Latin? Nothing doing. Monsieur loafs about, Monsieur hangs around, Monsieur talks, Monsieur writes poetry. And meanwhile, what am I doing? I'm working – yes, Monsieur! I run, I operate, I make calls, I see patients, I've got the hospital, all the red tape, the insurance forms and all that, I don't have a minute for myself, I eat fast, I don't sleep any more, I'm on the go night and day, I sacrifice myself for you, I give you my sweat and blood, I'm killing myself, I tell you seriously, my Benjamin, I'm killing myself for all of you, I'm killing myself for *you*!"

The big angry voice filled the study. The terrible blue eyes flashed in the red face. The doctor's shoulders heaved with indignation, fits of coughing racked him; now he was breathing hard, he was still bellowing, he was choking with rage. Standing before him, somewhat stooped, his hands open, Jean Calmet looked with despair at his master, who was in a trance. What was he to reply? That was the most painful of all: his father paralysed him. He would have liked to cry out to him that he was wrong. That he loved him. That he was pursuing his studies with some pleasure. That he immersed himself in the Latin authors with passion. That he was grateful to him for allowing him to work under pleasant conditions. But nothing came out of his mouth. Jean Calmet stood there stupidly, mute, looking obstinate and guilty, and it was precisely this which enraged the purple-faced doctor. Impossible to free himself from that hideous silence, to tell all at one fell swoop about his loneliness and confusion, impossible to throw his arms around the man's neck, to kiss him, to cry on those indestructible shoulders, glue his cheek to that rough cheek, as in bygone days feel the beard that scratches and scrapes his face, hear the strong voice in his throat by gluing his ear against the man's neck...

"Now, get the hell out of here, you little moron. You're as stupid as your brothers and sisters. And to think that, at fifty-eight years of age, I can't rely on anyone in this house!"

Fifty-eight years old. An old man. Nonsense. Jean Calmet remembered with extraordinary shame the vile story of Liliane. Liliane was a pretty girl from Paudex, even rather beautiful, with big brown eyes, a ponytail, tall, blooming, a bosom that moved in a bra plainly visible under her cotton-print blouse. Seventeen years old. A bit common, perhaps, her father a labourer, five or six kids crowded into the garret of a fisherman's shanty. Out of work, Liliane. A salesgirl's apprenticeship broken off after two months. She lolled about on the beach at Lutry, drank Coca-Colas while smoking cigarettes on the terrace of the Hôtel du Rivage. That is where Jean Calmet had met her; funny, round-breasted, broke; they saw each other again every afternoon of the long summer months, they went to the beach, they swam, they rented a boat, they rowed far out, they came back peacefully to the little shore... Liliane laughed, tanned herself, bloomed. Jean Calmet did not dare touch her breasts, he kissed her before her door, quickly; he waited for the next day's rendezvous with growing impatience. Liliane was always broke. At the end of the summer, her parents had insisted that she find another job as a salesgirl or as a supernumerary at the gas factory. Jean Calmet was upset at losing her. He had an idea. His father complained endlessly of being swamped with paperwork from his office, insurance forms that took for ever; then, too, the old servant was becoming incapable of performing correctly her work as receptionist. What if he hired Liliane? For once, the doctor had greeted the idea with satisfaction. Liliane began work at Les Peupliers on 30 August.

She changed at once. As early as the first week, although the doctor's office closed on Thursdays, she refused to go out with Jean Calmet on that day, and he had hung around her house sadly, alone, among the piles of sand and cement, in the harbour of Paudex that was under a fusillade of sunshine. Towards seven o'clock he finally saw her come home, he ran towards her, but she fled into her hallway, she quickened her steps; he called to her from downstairs:

"Liliane, Liliane, wait for me!"

She turned around and the look that she gave him was sad and full of shame. But he realized that only much later, remembering all the times that he had seen her, her pouts, her looks, her silences.

"Liliane!"

No answer. Those eyes. All their regret. The front door stands ajar, the evening sun pours into the cool hallway. Liliane is standing on a step in a flood of light that illuminates her violently, her bosom moves under the cloth, her bare legs shine... She turns around, she is swallowed up in darkness, Jean Calmet hears her running up the stairs. A door slams. Nightmare. He goes back out into the heat, he sees nothing, his eyes are full of tears, he goes back to Les Peupliers along the shore of the lake.

On the following days she kept on running from him. At Les Peupliers, he met her on the doorstep in the morning; he passed her in the vestibule, or, suddenly, while he was trying to read in the garden, her head would appear at one of the windows of the waiting room or the doctor's consulting room on the ground floor; she would come across him with a dazed astonishment, greet him painfully, and then the windowpane would sparkle at once, the window would close, and Liliane's image would disappear into the room. That lasted for a month. A month of embarrassment, of doubt, of impatience. Jean Calmet no longer ate. He slept badly. Or not at all. When he caught sight of Liliane at the end of a hallway, he would flee in his turn into a corner, as if he felt his own disgrace too shamefully to dare approach her directly. He hid from her. He suffered. But he suffered much more – in a more vile and permanent way – when he learnt the truth.

It was one fine autumn day, at the end of the afternoon. The visiting hours should have been over, and Jean Calmet needed to consult a dictionary that was kept in the doctor's office. He went down to the ground floor, somewhat ill at ease, and, as usual, he gave two quick knocks: no answer. He waited a few seconds, then he went in. To the right, the consulting room was empty. He started absently up the corridor, pushed open the office door, and the scene smacked him in the face: standing, her breasts bare, Liliane was pressing herself against the doctor, who was kissing her full on the mouth. Liliane's shoulders, torso, belly streamed with light; she turned, stupefied, and Jean Calmet, for the first time, saw the nipples on the girl's heavy, round bosom. The doctor was breathing hard. Nobody moved. A few seconds went by; no one spoke. Then Jean Calmet moved back a step and closed the door behind him. Dizziness seized him. One second. Two seconds.

"Shit!" cried the doctor's raucous voice from the other side of the wall.

Jean Calmet fled, shut himself up in his room and collapsed on a chair. That was almost twenty years ago. He was nineteen then; about to begin his second semester of his literature degree. Twenty years, and the sadness, the shame, the humiliation had not gone away. He recalled himself doubled over in his chair, motionless, silent, not even able to cry. And Liliane naked in the dazzling light.

And his father, red, panting, furious. And he, himself, stunned with pain. But why had Liliane given herself up so easily to that bastard? He would never know. He had seen her again a few days later, and this time she had not dared to avoid him. They had walked a hundred yards along the lake. Tense, strained, Jean Calmet:

"Liliane, have you slept with him?"

The coarse intonation of the reply still echoed in his ears:

"Well, you know, I lost my cherry. I had to lose it sometime, didn't I?"

He loved her. She was seventeen. He, nineteen. She was a woman. He, virgin, and wounded to the depths of his soul, frightened, not even finding anything to say that could communicate a little of his confusion and sadness. Nevertheless, he looked at her with intense curiosity: the spongy lips against her wide teeth, the curly forelock in her big eyes which no longer turned away, the brown neck in the blouse where her breasts lay heavy... Behind her, the seven o'clock sun set the lake ablaze, orange clouds ceased to move, fringed with liquid gold; white boats cruised out on the lake under the green slopes of Savoy. Who decides for us? Who triumphs in the beauty of the world? What anguish is to be drunk like a poison in that evening's light? Liliane was a woman and the doctor was her lover. His own father. Jean Calmet dug his nails into his palms. His own father had bitten that mouth. Tasted the smell of the nape of that neck. Grasped those pink-tipped breasts. Parted those tanned legs. Driven himself into that belly. The master had demanded his due. Had possessed. It was still going on. Everyone bent. Everyone yielded. He reigned. He fed on their submissiveness. And he had wanted that fresh flesh as a natural tribute to his power. That little girl belonged to him. She had yielded in his arms. She had moaned under his hands, panted under his unfailing strength. He was the father! The man of vigour, the owner, the law! Fifty-eight years of age. Seventeen years old. But the law… Jean Calmet immediately discarded the idea that this was the abduction of a minor: the doctor had not led this girl astray, had not seduced her. He had exercised a right. Who would ever contest it? Jean himself had yielded to that authority, he was ashamed of it, he was infuriated, but he bowed before his father's sovereign domination… A beautiful evening, to be sure. Green Savoy, the sky burning the lake like molten copper, and before it Liliane, who looks at him with a kind of tenderness, now, as if everything were still possible, as if their walks were going to resume. As if, after the father, the son in his turn were going to hurl himself on that meat. That awful word made Jean Calmet suffer at once. That meat? Who said such vile things? And he recalled his father, the infallible doctor, feeling flesh, grinding up fibres in small, sour apartments, in the morning, after the swaying elevator or the black staircase, when he accompanied him on calls to the homes of the poor, the humiliated, the wretched, who begged the master to give them enough to live on for a little while longer. Then Jean Calmet had had a kind of illumination: like a revelation that had driven him one notch surer into his loneliness. They too, the sick people, loved him. They adored him in their way. The doctor was generous. He was devoted. He came running. He came rushing. He fought against the insurance companies. He arranged their burials. He followed in the cortège. He spoke over their graves. To their greyish beds, only he brought noise, joking, all of the diversity of the outside. Liliane had been conquered by that power. And he, Jean, the poor dwarf? That beautiful girl was tender and unappreciated. Father a labourer. Mother a labourer. Too many kids in her room. And what future? A nervous, crazy student? The doctor radiated power. Now Jean Calmet looked at Liliane with tenderness. They were brother and sister, that sweet thing and he. They had gone through the same filth. Tyranny.

They could fight their way back to the surface. Meet again. Break out of that infernal circle. There would be a way out someday. The doctor would die. Then they would see who entered the true kingdom. *But my kingdom is not of this world?* With an extraordinary feeling of deliverance, Jean Calmet suddenly found himself open, light, completely cleansed of all anger. Of jealousy? She, he would coddle her later on. He knew it. He drove her to the back of his mind like an old fear. The sky was turning a golden grey. The lake was loaded with amber. Across the way, France was taking on reddish hues, shades of late autumn woods and squirrel fur. A smell of fish, blandly sickening and soothing, hung about the sewers of the bay of Lutry. A boat was drawing near the shore. People were milling around on a landing stage. Combat? A restless girl full of flavour stared into the depths of his eyes.

"Jean! I had to lose it sooner or later…"

He did not have the patience to wait. All of a sudden, he turned around, he started to run on the gravel of the jetty; sand crunched in his sandals like the last reminder of summer. Liliane! The summer! And Jean Calmet hurled himself like a madman into the tepid mist.

That is what he was remembering, seated at his big table before his books and his file cards, in the middle of that crowded night. He ran his hand over his throat: his beard was beginning to bristle again. Like on the faces of corpses… Wizened, Jean Calmet. Everything was all right. He rose, carefully checked the latch, the window, the electricity, brushed his teeth, shaved, showered, came back to hang around before the shelves of his bookcase, opened his leather-bound edition of Baudelaire, closed it again, drank a glass of Contrexéville, finding it as insipid as his life, came back to hang around Baudelaire, searched in a pile and found the photo by Nadar, felt the terrible curl of his lips like a sneer, recited to himself two verses of

Chant d'automne, shivered, switched off his lamp, opened the windows in the dark while one or two cars backfired behind idiotic gardens where stupid animals, porcupines as lost as himself, sucked in the last hydrocarbons of the damp urban air.

The ceremony of interring the ashes took place on Friday 20 October. It was the middle of the afternoon. The small sun yellowed the cemetery, where tufts of pinkish heather made rather dirty spots in the rays of light like bloodstains on amber-coloured linens. Jean Calmet met his mother in front of the crematorium; in a black astrakhan coat, she was pale and stooped. His brothers and sisters surrounded her. At four o'clock sharp the funeral director emerged in the central lane that bristled with crosses and elaborately decorated monuments, the black hat in his hand, and the crematorium official, also dressed and fitted with a hat of charcoal grey, joined them in the doorway of the chapel.

Both of them bowed before the widow, shaking her hand at great length, greeting each of the children with extreme solemnity.

"It's niche number 157," said the official. "The urn was brought this morning. As is customary, the ashes have been poured into it without the family's being present. Naturally, you can see them in a little while. If you'll be good enough to follow me…"

The meagre procession started into the cemetery, went up a lane, climbed up some steps bordered by boxwood, turned, took another lane between the graves and the shrubbery; finally they arrived before the columbarium, whose iron-latticed doors were open.

"Please go right in, Madame," said the official, motioning to the arched interior with his black hat.

Étienne took his mother's arm and they all started into the little building. The daylight filtered under the archway through tiny slits in the wall. Jean Calmet spun around: the walls were entirely partitioned with hundreds of numbered niches, the depth of which was hard to determine. One of them, at eye level, was sealed by a little black curtain fringed with silver: it bore the number 157, and they pointed it out to one another with their looks and their fingers. Then all became silent, and everyone stood motionless. The funeral director and the official advanced to the foot of the wall. On behalf of his company, the mortuary man reaffirmed his sympathy in a gentle voice. Then he pulled a paper from his pocket and read the municipal regulations on the storage of ashes in the columbarium. His paper refolded, the fellow stepped back a pace with a look of pained modesty.

Then the funeral director took up position beneath the black curtain and slowly, with weighty solemnity, his head straight, he uncovered the doctor's niche: the brocaded urn appeared, superb, luminous against its background of shadows, and everyone in the small gathering could read the inscription in light-coloured bronze capitals:

DOCTEUR PAUL CALMET
1894–1972

The letters and dates gleamed on the pebbled flanks of the vase. The man from the mortuary, having turned towards the family, pointed at the pigeonhole: all around it, above, to the side, below, other urns stood out against the black background of other niches, and it was like a strange assembly of round, motionless ghosts that stood guard, silently, within those cold walls. Jean Calmet shuddered. So that is the doctor's resting place for fifteen years. For all those years the doctor was going to remain motionless under that vault. Motionless? The urn was safely stowed away. But the official climbed up on a stepladder and took hold of the heavy vase with both hands. Now he carried it to Madame Calmet and raised the lid.

"You see, Madame. We have carefully done what was necessary. Your husband's ashes will be at your disposal whenever you want them. You can always cancel your contract by means of a simple letter, duly signed at our municipal office."

Then he carried the urn from one to the other; some touched it, leant over its gaping orifice and looked inside for a moment. Jean Calmet recoiled in horror when his turn came; the official stared at him curiously and went off to place the urn back in its niche.

They went out. It was cold. The sun was a red ball skimming thousands of bloodstained tombstones. They met before a bottle of white wine, and tea; the official and the man from the mortuary had followed; the Café du Reposoir was full of people in mourning, and Jean Calmet studied the boisterous scenes being indulged in, body and soul, by the families of the poor wretches who had just been shoved into a hole or roasted at a thousand degrees in a cast-steel machine. He did not accompany his brothers and sisters to Les Peupliers, where his mother invited them all to come for supper. He left them, full of remorse at having deserted them too soon on such an occasion, and he came back to the city streets with marvellous pleasure.

It was the hour when bands of boys and girls come down from the heights of Lausanne, where the schools and the faculties of the university are found, to the station from which they are going to take the trains all over the canton. How beautiful they are! thought Jean Calmet, who stopped in the middle of the Rue de Bourg and watched the swarming hordes of tanned kids. Lithe, solid, they hurried towards the station, speaking very loudly. Their splendour took his breath away, but he was pleased by this onslaught: slim, blond, helmeted with watered silk or braided locks like those of the Celts, with blue eyes, the youngsters bounded, chattering, the girls' breasts moving in their sweatshirts, in their long, purple or orange Indian dresses, and, although it was only the beginning of autumn, many of them were wearing high boots that gave them the bearing of innocently perverse and cruel conquerors. Excitement stirred Jean Calmet. His flesh was struck by the boys' strength and the sumptuous moistness of the girls. Those boys clad in tatters like guerrillas or like pals of Clint Eastwood, these magnificent bundles of health with their breasts bouncing, dressed in imitation leather or beautiful blue Levi's, Jean Calmet contemplated them with a tender fervour that cured him of the austerity of Lutry, of the affected politeness of the crematorium. They were far from his stifling family! Their old clothes affronted the doctor's voracious bonhomie. May they go on, may they continue, may they persevere, may they tear the place down, may they destroy these lousy families and these patriarchs and these tyrants and these big morons that have been paralysing us for centuries. Rage seized him, shook him. Then he began to smile again, because hundreds of other teenagers appeared in groups of three or four, their coats open on long legs, on solid thighs in worn denim, on flat bellies, belted with small iron and silver chains.

These merry barbarians were avenging him. They were not ones to quake before fathers or teachers. The thing that struck Jean Calmet was their health: they were all strong, loose-limbed, quick, and the tanned clearness of their skin, the transparency of their eyes, enchanted him. It was the same fascination that his students held for him: their beauty, their subtle, humorous animal nature gratified him mysteriously each moment of each lesson. They moved incessantly. They blew their noses in tissues that they dropped under their desks. The girls cleared their throats and scratched themselves like cowherds. They ran across the schoolyard shouting. They organized demonstrations at the drop of a hat: for peace in Vietnam, against the Israeli raids in Jordan, for sexual freedom, against Madame Golda Meir, against Nixon, to avenge the death of Amílcar Cabral. They handed out mimeographed flyers in the pouring rain, they peddled anti-nuclear posters in the icy north wind, they chanted ecumenical slogans in the snow; then they fought with snowballs, washed each other's faces with big melting handfuls, ran, collapsed over their desks like exhausted puppies.

Jean Calmet did not know that he had begun to smile. The crowd was still going by, the red and gold lighting of the storefronts made their hair shine, their teeth sparkle; badges blazed on their belts, pendants reflected the brilliance of the shop windows like mirrors. Jean Calmet was carried away with enthusiasm. In his flesh, he felt the radiating warmth of these boys and girls. Their blood flowed into his like a liqueur. He exulted. He began to laugh. Their eyes kindled his own gaze. Their breath revived his. Saps were seething in the boys. The girls secreted marvels. Jean Calmet gorged himself on both, fed, drank, strengthened himself. He recalled himself in class, after the lesson, when his students crowded around his desk, hemming him in their ring, sticking to him, leafing through his books, asking him questions, accompanying him to the Café de l'Évêché for the recess, which was spent drinking coffee, eating croissants amid the noise; then they went back up with him to the Gymnase and followed him to the door of the teachers' room, where Jean Calmet never made more than brief appearances, as his fellow teachers – despite the esteem in which he held them – seemed like so many censors placed, themselves, under the paternal authority of the principal, the supreme censor, whom Jean usually was afraid to meet. Still this feeling of being caught at fault, of being guilty... while the turbulent, frank boys and girls healed him of his anxieties and transfused their strength right into his heart.

Seven o'clock.

Jean Calmet remained standing on that pavement for a long time, admiring and dreaming. Now the groups were thinning out, the animation gave way to the felt-lined opulence of an elegant street where the fashionable dress shops and the show windows of jewellery stores came firmly back into power. Jean Calmet went to Le City to eat a pizza; he drank Chianti, ordered cheese, read the newspapers with tranquillity. Lonely? Not even that. He was haunted by those battalions of beautiful children. The urn was officially, municipally, contractually sealed behind the high iron gate of the columbarium. In short, order reigned. He had to get used to this calm happiness. The winter was going to be long and mild. Jean Calmet imagined himself a fox, a marten, perpetual savage snug in his burrow while, outside, the snow is falling, falling on the fields and forests. Chimneys began to smoke in the dells. The sky was black against the hills, a car went by on the icy road... Winter was setting in. But what winter? It was only October, and this day had carried Jean Calmet far from his prisons. He listened to the copper autumn, the furrowed, rotting autumn, give way to the great white peace. Deserted depths opened up in the countryside, where gatherings of motionless birds, wood owls, great-horned owls, and stags, wild boars, badgers, animals from bygone eras that had persevered, that had stubbornly persisted deep in the woods, spoke to him in their sly tongue. Their primal language! Jean Calmet listened to them searching with their snouts, scratching with their hooves, digging defences in the ground. Claws seized, beaks cut into the flesh of panic-stricken field mice, flights of smoke spread their networks between the guardian trees.

* * *

Every morning Jean Calmet hesitated between his two razors: the Gillette and the electric shaver. When he was not feeling well, not sure of himself, he used the electric one, which spared him from having to use water, an added advantage. When he felt strong he used the Gillette. Since the interment of the urn at the columbarium, he had decided to eliminate the controversy and use the blade every morning, *naturally*. For too long, the Gillette had been challenging him. Frightening him, pushing him around from the bottom of its blue case. But once the decision had been made and held, he had to handle the razor cautiously: the object was endowed with very obvious powers, and its ability to stir up memories was ironically inexhaustible. At the sight of it, on touching it, ghosts loomed up, and one of them made the bathroom, the apartment and, more seriously, Jean Calmet's whole mind echo with its terrible, furious voice. Hundreds of times, as a child, Jean Calmet had watched his father shave. He would sit on a wooden stool, two or three steps from the doctor, and he never tired of watching him lather his face with precise, revolving little strokes, which concealed it bizarrely in the white foam. Often the doctor would turn around and, in jest, suddenly stretch out his arm: with a stroke of his shaving brush he would soap the nose of Jean Calmet, who kept the fragrant puff stuck to his skin as long as possible. Then came the whetting on a kind of cradle set in a flat steel box, and with the razor finally loaded, the operation would begin. The doctor would begin dramatizing immediately. He mimed pain, twisted his mouth with two fingers of his left hand, emitted strange moans while attacking his chin, and if he cut himself (which was frequent because of his excitement and haste) he would hold out the reddened pad of cotton to Jean Calmet, bend over him, offer him his throat, make him touch the wound from which oozed a thin, crimson thread that branched out over the brown skin in small, star-shaped channels. Then his father cried, screamed, gasped, feigning suffering, and although he knew that this was a scene which recurred like a ritual in their father-and-son relationship, the child could not help suffering, becoming apprehensive, and he remained strongly affected all day after the doctor's tragicomic gesticulation. When he was old enough to shave, he wanted a Gillette just like his father's. Made of silver! In the same blue case! And this morning, he stared at it glumly, that case where the sacred object lay hardening. He stretched out his hand towards the glass shelf under the mirror, which reflected his image too clearly. He opened the case: the razor gleamed in the silk. Blackish silver. He took it in his left hand and, with his right, turned the round screw at the end of the handle, the screw controlling the two plates clamping the blade: it appeared, dark blue, the cutting edges white, gleaming, and which would gleam all the more in a few minutes when he honed them on the block of leather in the cradle. Jean Calmet removed the blade and held it, cold and blue, between two fingers, like a foreboding of night. He put the razor back, he raised the thin blade towards the window: it lived with an extraordinarily concentrated and autonomous life. With a violent life. Jean Calmet went on looking at it for a few moments, then he set it on the cradle, honed it for a long time on both sides, put it back in the razor with respect.

Saturday 21 October: it was his last morning's classes before the autumn vacation. Everything pointed to fine weather for the end of October. There would be walks, dreamy strolls on back roads, scenery. Jean Calmet promised himself several times to go up into the Jorat valley to see the forest, the prairies. He would read. He would make notes while preparing his lessons for after the holidays. He shaved peacefully, dried the blade, replaced the razor in its little case: in the back of his memory he clearly made out his father's face.

Sun, a tang in the air; the trees in the parks were turning brown against the blue. Jean Calmet loved the morning. The town had been cleaned. Flights of sparrows swooped down, cheeping, onto the pavements; at the red lights, through the open window, he perceived their steady cries like a funny, happy promise. Behind the cathedral, the soft gold of the oaks in the Sauvabelin forest could be seen, and the smoke from small factories went straight up into the silken sky, as in the paintings of Lausanne from the last century, in their ornate frames in the antique shops of the Cité quarter. A squad of good-humoured gendarmes came out of the barracks building and, roaring with laughter, piled into two trucks. Once, early in the morning, at the foot of the sandstone towers, the workers from the archaeological department laid out the skeletons of Burgundian monks beside open graves, solemn-faced photographers busied themselves at setting up tripods and taking measurements under the curious looks of passers-by. Yesterday, Jean Calmet gazed for a long time at the grins of skulls, the holes for eyes; a girl from the university cleaned the sand of the grave from the skeleton's teeth with precise little strokes of her brush. They explained to him that they were remains from the late Middle Ages: a cemetery on the hillside: the church is built over the graves; on the north-east side leans the cemetery of the cloister which has just been opened and photographed. Jean Calmet bent anxiously over the skeletons: intact, and that silent laugh of the jawbones... One of his students slipped a sprig of geranium into the corpse's big, gasping mouth. For an instant the blonde tresses of the little Burgundian girl brushed across the bones of the saint that had emerged from eternity.

Jean Calmet parked his car in the courtyard of the Gymnase. Groups of girls and boys were seated on the stone benches. The bell rang. He climbed the stairs to his classroom with François Clerc, one of his colleagues. He was fond of François Clerc, an independent fellow who had published some poems and who taught French. François stopped on the last step:

"You want to get together one day next week? We can go for a ride. You could take me along in your car and we could have a drink up along the Broye, what do you say?"

A calm, happy smile, and François Clerc's grey eyes that said: "Say yes, you haven't been yourself for some time, this ride will do you good, and I feel like going too." They promised to call each other after Monday; they walked a little further down the hallway, where tardy students were running to their classes, then they shook hands. Jean Calmet went into his classroom.

They had reached the Broye by back roads, and, once again, Jean Calmet was overwhelmed by the beauty of the land-scapes. The pine trees mingling with the oaks and aspens raised black tapers in the red copper of the foliage. Meadows were turning rosy under the grey sun. Gentle, solemn flocks crossed the pastures with the tinkling of bells as in childhood poems. Villages with a pointed steeple loomed up among the hills, red tiles, low houses, farms like castles. The car passed tractors pulling tons of beets and sacks of potatoes lined up like monks on the deck of the wagons. The driver raised his hand in greeting, kids in overalls waved a scarf or cap. Thierrens, Molondin, Combremont, the country became more undulating, more secret; the road buried itself in green, deserted regions, the forests on the foothills were dense and dark, flights of crows swooped down on the slopes. Jean Calmet loved those lonely spots with their legends, and with foxes running under the orange moon. He drove without haste, and by mutual consent the two friends remained silent. That autumn day gripped them: the grass dotted with autumn crocuses, the pearls of mist in the grey, the birds, the bronze hedgerows, the roads that vanish into the bristling forest, the smoke from fires on the grassy banks where standing road workers drink beer and pass around cigarettes, laughing. They went down towards the Broye: it shone behind willows in the centre of a slack, green plain. Further on, the phosphorescent mist. They saw the water of the river palpitating among the branches and rushes; the current fled, sparkling; the whole countryside was relieved by its cool delicacy. An intoxication overcame Jean Calmet, lifted him; he looked at the road, the river, the woods, the whole background of the scenery under its layer of gauze, with marvellous pleasure. With the car parked under a poplar, the two friends made their way to the bank of the river and sat down. Noon. The bells of villages began ringing at full peal. Jean Calmet imagined the dance of the bronze belfries, all the small, cobblestoned squares before each church, the arched doors open in the soft light of the street, and, in the doorway, a striped cat licks itself clean and falls asleep...

François Clerc stretched out in the cropped grass. He closed his eyes. Jean Calmet watched the delicate face give itself up by degrees to relaxation. The stain of his beard circled his mouth. In turn, he lay down on the grassy bank. He felt the cold of the ground on his shoulders, and the grass, sharp and dry, pricked his neck. François smoked. He was singing softly. Jean Calmet also whistled the little tune; the sun was driving off the mist, the Alps of Fribourg appeared, dazzling, in the blue sky. His eyes closed for a moment, Jean Calmet listened to the Broye run. It was a lively, silky sound: a constant rending, as if the water were breaking itself, cutting itself, coming asunder indefinitely; at the same time the current caressed the grassy shore and the gentle seething wistfully tore itself away from the gorges, from the hollows, from the scars of the bank. Jean Calmet knew himself to be the brother of that water: it ran within him, it crossed him, it carried him across the plain towards the wooded hills, the grasslands, the German towns, the Rhine... François Clerc gave himself a shake, sat up; the two friends talked for a quarter of an hour in the sun. Then they went to Lucens, following the Broye, and they entered an inn for lunch. It was the Café du Chemin de Fer: a long room broken in two by a strange angle, the proprietress young and provocative, the French waitress with a high-pitched voice; the lone customers ate at small tables, travelling salesmen, railway employees in blue smocks and – right up against the bar – the bellowing table of tipsy card-players. The French girl swung between the tables, swore at her customers, burst out laughing. Jean Calmet ate with tranquillity: the wine was good, the roast had the taste of thyme and laurel, the conversation took a happy turn that enchanted the friends. François told the annoying story of what had recently happened to one of their fellow teachers at the Gymnase: he had begun writing letters to two of his students, two inseparable friends (who were something of outsiders and sophisticates); at first, innocent notes, then rascally ones, more and more explicit lines of verse. A few suppers had followed: the pretty ones went to them in rather scanty attire and then boasted about it. The class – which did not like that teacher – had begun to grow restless. François recounted the principal's inquiry and the teacher's reaction, rather shamefaced and chastised. One of the poems had made the rounds of the schoolyard, and François recited it, roaring with laughter.

> *Ne soyez cruelle blondine,*
> *Et vous perfide brunette...*

The students had laughed, too. The principal had not taken it in quite the same way. He had carried out an investigation and had made threats.

"The guy lost his head," said François Clerc. "He became panic-stricken. In the end, he gave himself away. He didn't know what to do after all that. The story came out last week. You'll see, when we come back after the holiday, the whole Gymnase will know about it. I feel sorry for him, that poor Verret. Poor old fascist. And, to top it off, with that face of his…"

And it was true that Verret had a singular skull and torso, as if it were all welded together in one piece. He looked like a short, fat frog buttoned up tight in grey-green policeman's shirts. But he would roll nice, big, restless eyes that touched Jean Calmet. Was it true that he had been fired from a boarding school for sodomy? No one knew much about his private life: supposedly, he had married an Austrian or German girl – nobody knew which – a girl much younger than he was. In his locker in the teachers' room he had tacked up the photo of Gudrun Ensslin, the terrible mistress of Baader, which he had cut out of *Stern*. A hard, sensual face under a blonde helmet. She had done the shooting, bumped guys off, "cased" banks. A pastor's daughter, of course. Verret had had her as a student for a whole winter at a Stuttgart high school. She was seventeen. Then the debauch, crime, the Baader gang, assassinations with hand grenades, the newspapers…

And Verret remained that curious mixture of pride and humiliation, parading around with his frog face and his trousers that were too short, sighing dejectedly, staring at everyone with his big pathetic eyes; and fleeing sideways to treat himself to a glass of kirsch at the Café de l'Évêché to try to buck up his spirits. What did Verret dream about in front of his drink? About Baader's gun moll? About the pastor's daughter from Stuttgart whom he had got to recite Lamartine? About the boys of the Legion of French Volunteers against Bolshevism that he might have despaired of ever joining in the flatlands of Pomerania? About the shorts and pyjamas of the boarding school? About the two chicks who had led him on, then dropped him, after the

71

incident of the suppers? Undoubtedly about all of that, at once, slowly, the way one chews nostalgia, and the bitterness of the thin soup would make him lower his broad forehead to the red tablecloth. He worshipped German. Often, Jean Calmet had spoken to him about the poets, and Verret, lighting up with a strange tenderness, had quoted snatches of Schiller, Heine, Kleist and Jünger. One evening, when they had met rather late, they went to drink beer in a smoky café. His eyes glowing, Verret had whispered Goethe as a girl went by, a very young, surprised creature whose lover dragged her around by the arm in the noisy crowd:

> *Du liebes Kind, komm', geh mit mir*
> *Gar schöne Spiele spiel' ich mit dir…*

and, instantly, his face faded, a look of heavy sadness settled on his features, and, without embarrassment, Jean Calmet had placed his hand over his colleague's square hand.

"Do you think he'll hold out?" François Clerc asked suddenly, jerking Jean from his reverie. "He's absolutely mad."

"Most of all, I think he's suffering," said Jean Calmet, who remembered Verret's gaze. "He's a very bright, very lonely guy. He's been unlucky. Nobody's giving him a helping hand. We're all treating him like bastards. You and I should encourage him when school starts again. See him now and then. Defend him."

And he promised himself – whatever the attitude of François – to see Verret regularly from the next week on. But the memory of his colleague hung around him like remorse. The wine made him slightly drunk. He rose, excused himself and went to the men's room.

The corridor was dank. Jean Calmet went along it without haste, glad to be alone for a moment. Flakes of plaster were peeling off the walls, and mildew had formed on those spots. Just beside the door of the men's room, he stopped, gripped by the sudden discomfort into which he had been thrown by what he saw – what he began to look at with his eyes popping out of his head: exactly at the side of the door, across from him, arriving without haste at the end of the hallway, waiting for him in the whitish light of a naked square to trap him, tear him, defy him, stood a rusty umbrella stand in which only a single cane – an insignificant, useless object – turned its curved handle towards Jean Calmet. Insignificant, of course, for everyone, that old thing. A bit of wood to be thrown into the garbage, or be burned, or be got rid of with the rusty scrap iron that held it and against which one might stub one's toe, hurt oneself. Meanwhile, that filthy thing might have been there for years, and Jean Calmet could not tear his gaze from its detestable bulges. It was a knotty walnut cane with a braided look, about four feet in length, which shot at him its big handle ending in a thick bud, a particularly visible acorn from which Jean Calmet could no longer take his eyes. Why was he thinking of his father's penis? What demon was haunting that corridor or that umbrella stand or that WC whose trickling sent cold chills down his back, what bad genii had he disturbed, behind the mildewed patches of the walls, for his fear and his aversions to freeze him immediately like a guilty thing in that wan light? His father's penis was extended towards him above the pitted ring of the umbrella stand, first the budding, greyish glans, then the swollen organ, knotted, knobby, bent, that use had strengthened, polished, without taking away any of its thick aggressiveness. Jean Calmet tried to reassure himself by looking at the shaft of the cane, following it up to its end, which was tipped with blackish rubber in the shadow of the umbrella stand. Wasted effort, quickly he went back up the shank as far as the swelling, up to that protruding, gleaming head that turned itself towards him from the bottom of what ironic nothingness? His father's penis forgotten in a hallway deep in the valley of the Broye: he *would* have to come just this way, and, absently, soothed, enter this out-of-the-way café and feel good in it; walk down this corridor unknown to the whole world without turning his eyes away from the details of its humble adornment; finally come across that umbrella stand where the doctor was waiting for him, reminder, burst of laughter, injury. And now, paralysed, ensnared, Jean Calmet was panting slightly before his father's turgescent glans! He moved forward a trembling hand, restrained himself, then with index finger and thumb he touched the hard organ, let his fingers run over its knots, came back to the protruding knob. Exorcism? he wondered. He was ashamed, he felt a kind of horror for his act, he went on touching. All of a sudden, as if he had received an electric shock in his palm, he let go of the cane and shut himself up in the men's room. His face was grey in the mirror. Then he rejoined François Clerc, who was quietly reading the local paper.

A few hours later, lying flat on his bed, his armpits and forehead running with sweat, Jean Calmet dreamt ominously of a grassy field, on a considerable slope, where a certain buffalo with flaring horns charged at anything that moved around them. A certain African bullock, still hard to see, but its eye was bloodshot, its horns made a sharp lyre, its body flared out paradoxically into a yellow ball, which at each bounce became harder and struck the passer-by viciously. In his turn, Jean Calmet ventured into a vacant patch of ground at the foot of a cliff. The horned ball aimed at him, reared, charged, struck him hideously. Jean did not cry out. An umbrella stand picked him up, hugged him in its rusty ring... He awoke as one might go through a door: his father was sitting in an armchair across from his bed. No. It was a heap of file folders topped by an old photo from a holiday. He got up like a spring: he lay down again, stretched himself without pleasure. Nevertheless, he imagined the cool well-being of the urns in the columbarium of Montoie. Immediately cooings enchanted him. Rustlings of feathers. Golden, tepid caresses. Downy embraces, mossy, amorous shamming, quarrelsome feints, bounds, flights, attacks, odd leaps, oblique returns, holds clenched with pink-beaded feet, thrusts by sharpened beaks of grey gold, spitting, pecking conversations, coated tongues, courtesans' kisses, pecks.

The whole crypt awakened. The bodies rose all at once out of their ashes. There were gentle, silken, tender bodies like the sensual birds of his visions. There were hard bodies. Censors. Auditors. There were also white shapes hoisted above their vases like lone gigantic worms, and Jean Calmet would have wished to scream with compassion at the spectacle of those phosphorescent forms topped by a perfectly recognizable face.

Then sleep came over him again. He saw a chimney smoking in the middle of a mausoleum that was sunlit and covered with celestial blue. He went through a country of rivers where schoolyards full of tireless adolescents opened before him. He was met by an irascible bull. And, as usual in his dreams, the monster stared at him from the top of a hillock, or from a slope, or from an abyss, and suddenly its bulk smashed Jean Calmet, who persisted in living through this adventure with a bit of humour, and a moral stubbornness that must have been inspired by the gods. Those gods who watch over the happiness of little men, from the black shore of their sorrow to the white shore, where the waves play like flashing knives.

Part II
The Spirit of Dionysus

Why did the knees prevent me?
Or why the breasts that I should suck?

Job 3:12

T HERE WAS CHRISTMAS.
He dug himself in.

He wrapped himself in the cocoon of convention, his family's customs, the somewhat fishy tepidness of Lutry, his mother's uneasy affection, the music, the meals, the bells. There was the Christmas tree as each year, as there had always been. There were his sisters, his brothers, the cries of his overexcited nephews, the melancholy of gifts, the eyes shining with tears in the light of candles. There was the father's empty chair. There was the big clock standing in its coffin behind the ghost.

There was 31 December.

He went to bed.

The next day, he strolled along the lakeside. Still that rather sickening sweetness of the shore grown tepid in the winter sun. Mimosas bloomed in gardens. In vaguely opaque greenhouses gleamed carnations, begonias, cyclamens, reddish stains, a bit frightening, like bloodstained cotton wads under the hot glass. Palm trees rose in the blue sky among pines and plane trees with bare branches. People dawdled on the tree-lined avenues. On the embankment at Lutry, they were already having their aperitifs in the open air, and the women had those open, pulpy lips that you see them with in the spring, on the pavement cafés of La Côte.

Jean Calmet stopped at Les Peupliers to see his mother, then walked back to Lausanne. He thought about the old house under the trees. What silence, today, in the big sunlit room where his mother spent her days between the clock and the glittering lake facing Savoy. Tender pity came to him for that grey woman with nothing to do, helpless, who trotted from the kitchen to her armchair, a teapot in her hand; then she poured his tea warily and nibbled salted breadsticks, apologizing for making too much noise with her new dentures.

He had never known this woman. Compassion seized him. She, too, she more than any of them, had bent under the tyrant, had been broken, destroyed. She was silent. But her sad smile told all. She had not complained once, and the doctor's absence left her deserted like a ruined city. She had opened old photo albums. She had not cried. But she stayed in her armchair, the album open on her lap, her gaze fixed, lost in the light from the window that she did not see, studying the ghostly presences that had peopled her past. Oh the destiny of a deprived Samaritan. A nurse forgotten in the depths of an abandoned hospital. Just then, evening was falling over Lutry; she must still be in the same spot, under the red bars of the setting sun, her gaze motionless before her cold teapot, Madame Jeanne-Aimée Calmet, née Rossier. She came from the isolated country, at the foot of the Jura mountains; she had been a maidservant, she had left the farms, the pastureland, the sheep runs, she had become his father's servant. Jeanne! My glasses! Jeanne! My bag! My cane! A mug of coffee! And those lousy kids that you're raising all wrong. And those meals that I won't come to eat. Wait for me. You are made to wait for me, Jeanne. Your hands have stirred the soup, cooked the meat, opened the bottle. I won't come. I'm roaming. I'm the master. I open bellies. I search through flesh. I cut. It's me who threatens, who consoles, who heals, me who gives hope, me who keeps vigil at the door of the realm of death. Death, that miserable thing, doesn't dare show itself! It falls back when I come, it beats a retreat, it buries itself in its domains! I cut, I pinch, I search, I set right, I tie up, I tear off, I sew up again, I'm a tireless soldier, a mercenary, a legionnaire; get out of here, Death, you don't scare me. Do you understand? Leave me alone with your timetables and your pitiable looks, I have every right, me, the warrior, the master of life. You wait for me and submit to me. Jeanne cleans the untouched table and lies down alone in the big bed. Jeanne spends the summer waiting for the doctor, who is always on the move, waging war. The children come back, go off again, the summer ends, time ensnares itself in autumn, the lake smells of rotting fish on the edge of winter, Jeanne readies the house for the celebrations of Christmas, New Year's Eve, she looks at the old photos. Jeanne Calmet. My mother. I was her Benjamin, her baby, her consolation and her joy. Her green grass. Her fresh air. I escaped in my turn. I didn't return to Les Peupliers. I'll come back more often. Her consolation. Her joy. I will outlive her. She will die in the room with the big bed, slight, shrunken on the pile of her pillows, white pillows from the song. Goodbye, Mother, gentle girl from the field of snow. You will be burned. There will be the same flowers, the same wreaths as in the month of September. The same faces at the services. We'll have the same snack at the Café du Reposoir, white wine, tea, breadsticks, sweet wafers, and during the week, one fine evening, your children will sit at the table at Les Peupliers, around a mortuary catalogue from which they will select your urn. Goodbye, Mother, sweet austere woman of the Jura, you went to church trembling and the sky fell on your head...

There was the new school term in January.

Teachers' meetings, piles of translations to be corrected. Flat boredom.

A month went by. Nothing to be said. Then it was 21 February, and Jean Calmet met the Cat Girl.

Then he could believe that the spirit of Dionysus had entered him.

It was five o'clock in the afternoon.

On the doorstep of the Café de l'Évêché, Jean Calmet saw the Cat Girl sitting in the seat that he liked. He took a few steps towards her, as if he too were going to sit near the window, in the angle where the light is soft and clear. The Cat Girl! She had not looked at him. But he had given her that name right away, it was law and magic, right away she had plunged him into the mad, mysterious joy of Dionysus. She wore a coat lined with yellow and white cat fur, open over a whole intricacy of necklaces. Her hair spilt out of a yellow and white fur hat. Golden hair, bronzed hair. She was knitting with white wool, her face bent towards her work; she had removed several rings in order to work more easily and the gems, the rings of blackish metal shone on the red tablecloth before her, where a half-consumed cup of milk also stood.

He had never seen her. Perhaps he would never see her again. He sat down at a nearby table, across from her. His heart pounding, happiness in his soul, he looked at her, he looked at her intensely, he felt cascades gushing deep within him; precipices opened up in his bones, sonorous, where age-old stones fell. The mountain wind whistled in the pines, the sea wind assailed the fig trees. He found himself borne by those forces, lifted, hurled; sap bounded into his blood, new humours shook him, starry skies, volcanos in flames, springs, storms, stampedes of horned herds, leaps of goats on slopes made wild with the smells of flowers; all these images seized him, went through him, came back to be swallowed up in him, threw him into a motionless, magnificent trance.

The Cat Girl lifted her eyes. Joy and burning! She rested her gaze on him: two emeralds ringed with copper that gleamed deeply in the late afternoon light.

She was still looking at him: to his own amazement he spoke to her first.

"That's pretty, what you're knitting. It looks soft..."

The Cat Girl was not surprised. She smiled, and her answer was as simple as her appearing there was marvellous.

"It's knitting," she said. And she continued to smile.

Jean Calmet noticed that, when smiling, like a cat, she ran the tip of her pink tongue over her lower lip, which began to shine.

"What a light," he said, and he stretched himself, while noise-makers, marching bands, fires, drums crackled and resounded deep in his skull, making a great whirling festival.

"You like that yellow sky too?" asked the Cat Girl, who placed her knitting on the table and slipped her rings back on, massaging the joints.

"That yellow sky," said Jean Calmet, "that yellow sky and that pink sky. Agate... It's as warm as spring."

And instantly he saw buds burst open, sap running over tree trunks covered with bees, fawns cowering in the dense hay. The miracle lasted. The Cat Girl stared at him tranquilly, as if she wanted to fix his features in her memory, and her attention did not embarrass Jean Calmet; on the contrary, he felt pleasure at being studied by that green eye spangled with light, which showed its curiosity without haste. He exulted. The red tablecloths kindled glowing fires along the walls. Rays of sunlight, where the cigarette smoke danced, striped the penumbra up to the bar. A grotto hubbub full of tenderness and passion cheered the heart. What power emanated from this girl? What enchanter had provided her with that power, near this window, in this café where Jean Calmet spent several hours each day? The sun placed orange bars on the rooftops of La Mercerie; the cathedral was a torch before the sky. The Cat Girl finished her milk; once again the pink tongue ran over the slightly swollen mouth.

"Do you come to this café often?" asked the Cat Girl.

He was expecting that question: as if its banality were the sign of an extraordinary understanding between the apparition and himself.

"I come here every day," said Jean Calmet. "I've never seen you…"

"I'm from Montreux. Today I rented a room in this neighbourhood."

Jean Calmet would have liked to ask why she had left Montreux, what she had come to do in Lausanne. But he knew that those things would be revealed to him. The enchantment did not stop: Montreux with its solar palaces in their gardens of fig and orange trees, Montreux with its pearled turbans and Rolls-Royces across from the saw-toothed Alps, a town that a number of prodigies are metamorphosing into a surrealist cemetery, into an Anglo-Balkan postcard, into a haven for baroque theatre, into a brochure for the Orient Express, into a worldly Swiss Ali Baba's cave! And the Cat Girl had just left that exotic reserve, aided by the spirits of the mountains and the water that inspired her and protected her like their mysterious child!

The Cat Girl had put all her rings back on, the Afghan rings, the Arab rings. She tossed her knitting and skeins of yarn helter-skelter into a little basket, she slid over the bench all the way along the table and rose.

"Are you coming?" she said simply.

Jean Calmet put some change on the red tablecloth and followed her. He opened the door for her, and the setting sun haloed them with its crimson sparks. Towards the city, the Bessières bridge was burning. All the windows on the Rue de Bourg were Archimedes' mirrors. The tower of l'Évêché, a square, dark mass against the sky, was crowned with charred timbers like the ruins of the castles of the heretics, and, before them, the cathedral, a sheaf of wax tapers and pink cannons, hurled its rockets into the sky.

They walked in the direction of La Cité. Jean Calmet looked at the Cat Girl's little round basket with gentle exasperation. She swung it against him, at arm's length; it was all childhood, that basket, the treasure of Little Red Riding Hood in the forest, the baggage of dreams, the solicitude of mothers for lonely grandmas, and, in her little boots, a girl starts trotting under the big trees and night falls and the woods grow thicker and the wolf comes. The Cat Girl, too, she would bring her galette and her little jar of butter deep in the woods. Her present. Or has she already delivered it?

She stopped before a door on the Rue de la Cité-Devant.

"It's here," she said, and he followed her into a narrow hallway that smelt of wet cement. The timer on the hall lights was ticking away. She stopped at the second landing.

"It's here," she said again, and he went behind her into a large room that the red evening flooded.

A bed, a chair. At the foot of a wall an open suitcase where clothes and sheaves of paper were piled up. The bells of the cathedral began to strike six. He had known the Cat Girl for one hour, and already she busied herself in the kitchen; he heard her moving cups, filling a pot.

"You aren't bored, are you?" she shouted at him. "Take a look out of the window – it's pretty."

Pretty, it was the courtyard of the Gymnase, the big esplanade lined with elm trees, and, behind them, harmonious, the old Bernese façade under its turret and its great roof of brown tiles. The windows of the principal and the secretary's office were still lit. Jean Calmet came back into the room and sat down on the only chair. Then the Cat Girl brought a little coffee pot and two tiny cups on a tray.

She still had her angora hat on her head and her coat of yellow and white skin.

"Get out of there," she said gaily. "You're taking up the only table in the house!"

She placed the coffee pot and the tray on the chair, and Jean Calmet sat on the bed. It was a big bed covered with a gilded spread. He sank into it with happiness. The Cat Girl took off her coat and hung it at the window. She served the coffee in the dolls' cups and sat down next to Jean Calmet on the big bed.

"I'm glad it's you," she said. "I've been here since early this afternoon, I needed somebody for the house-warming. I'm glad it's you. Your health!"

"Your health," said Jean Calmet, and he looked at the room full of red sun the way a Welsh cabin boy studies the hold of a galleon from the Indies. The empty room that the last rays gorged with rubies and copper. They drank their coffee. Night fell. Jean Calmet did not feel the need to speak. He was borne by cool sweetness. The Cat Girl did not light her only lamp. When he knew that all the intensity of the mystery and tenderness would not disappear, he left her: in her doorway, she drew close to him, her arms glued to her body, her gaze questioning.

"Yes," said Jean Calmet. "I'll come back."

She came closer still; he breathed an odour of cinnamon mixed with cool night, a little sweat, pollen, he felt her long hair against his neck, against his cheek. Then he bent towards her and, on her forehead, as one might reassure a little girl before the darkness, he placed a brief kiss which made them both shiver.

In the days that followed, a host of objects arrived to fill up the Cat Girl's red room and the gilded bed. First, there was a yellow stone, big as a man's fist, that she wanted on the only chair, beside the bed. Then there were swan feathers on the pillow. Then came an unsteady little chest, and on the chest, some oak leaves, a five-bladed penknife, postcards from before 1914, a pocket watch with a broken crystal, an old tea can on which one saw the picture of a castle and a little lake under a hill covered with heather. Then there was a black-painted rocking chair, a small bench, a round cushion on the bench, on which the Cat Girl had crocheted a purple snail.

"I'm furnishing the place!" she said, laughing. But nothing seemed less weighty than the booty that she brought back from her outings. The feathers and the leaves fluttered. The chest looked like something from a doll's house. The yellowing postcards came from the back room of Melusina's shop. The yellow rock cast gleams like the philosopher's stone. The rocker invited children in high shoes, on the porch of a bungalow, to rock themselves endlessly before a big garden full of catalpas where a stream reflecting daffodils ran. The bench awaited a parasol bearer.

"Where do you make your finds?" asked Jean Calmet.

"I don't know. At the marketplace. At the Salvation Army! You ought to come with me. They've got everything in their store. There's an old sergeant who's seen me a lot for a week now, she gives me discounts; it's nice, she put an army overcoat away for me. A corporal's hooded coat, with stripes, the belt at the back and everything! And the federal cross on the brass buttons, you see how beautiful it will be?" Jean Calmet loved that gaiety. And the fact that she dawdled around all day. He asked her:

"What did you do this afternoon?"

"I was knitting in a café."

"Which café?"

"I don't know. Not a very big café, not a very small one, near the Place de la Riponne. It was brown. I was talking to some guy, he was sad, he bought me tomato juice."

"And after that?"

"After that I went for a walk in a supermarket. I looked at the posters."

So it was. She dreamt. She stopped. She started again. When he came back to her place on the day after their first meeting, Jean Calmet wanted to know what she did, what she lived on. She did not answer that type of question. She had a little bit of money, her room was supposed to be paid for by relatives. But what relatives? She remained evasive, she dreamt again, she imagined odd, mysterious relationships, disinterested ones, returns to a shiny past, trips into other lives, islands in time, voyages. Everything was made up and everything was true in those stories. She levitated, but in an obvious, sweet happiness that continued to bewitch Jean Calmet. Who is she? he wondered during the day. He taught his classes; a growing impatience took hold of him, threw him into confusion, and, when the pink and yellow hour came at the end of the afternoon, he heard Dionysus' torches sputter; the landscape burst into flame, the torrents seethed, women – dishevelled, slimy with juice and sunlight – leapt in echoing vats, and Jean Calmet found, once more, that burning joy which had seized him the minute he had laid eyes on the Cat Girl.

She was named Thérèse Dubois. Her father had died in a mountain-climbing accident. She had begun studying at the Beaux-Arts. Regained her freedom. She went home to Montreux on Saturdays, spending Sundays with her mother. Thérèse was the Cat Girl. It was law. Magic. And what curiosity would be worth this joy?

One evening, Jean Calmet found her tacking up a huge poster over her bed. A bristling animal – a cat, a furry girl, a panther crouching to spring from the depths of a forest or from an abyss, or from a set of black walls on which its ghostly reflection trembled. Thérèse, standing on the bed with its gilded spread, was unrolling the print which she had managed to secure by the upper edge, on the left and on the right, but the photograph coiled itself back up capriciously, the panther's paws ended up comically on its head, the dark opening behind her grew smaller, filled with wrinkles, tautened like Balzac's *Peau de Chagrin* that a wicked enchanter had turned inside out on her like a glossy black coif. But the Cat Girl's left hand succeeded in securing the wild roll, and two firm little fingers seized a thumbtack balanced on an upraised knee. The joints grew white in the effort of her finger to sink the tiny barb into the wall. A double operation. Now the Cat Girl moved back one step, two steps, she ran a caress over the smooth surface, and the feminine animal, the tigress-girl, the little female ghoul sprung from the erased prison, reflected her in the black mirror of the paper.

"It's pretty," said the Cat Girl.

"It's pretty," said Jean Calmet. And he sat down in the rocking chair with perfect happiness. Joy and courage! The little tray, the coffee pot from the fairy tale, the dwarfish cups. And you, coffee, in our breasts. In our neighbouring, linked bellies, and each of us drinks his little cup like a miraculous crater...

One evening Jean Calmet masturbated and was ashamed to see Thérèse again, staring at him with her pure eyes. She had her complicated necklaces, her rings, and on her head a tiny iron chain fastened a transversal braid. Jean Calmet remembered his father's gaze: does the sweet sorceress know? He was overcome with curiosity: and what about her – is her hand taut, her finger gluey in the nocturnal milk? The lights of the Café de l'Évêché began to circle with mystery the faces of lone drinkers, as if the wooden panels behind them were burning black, like impenetrable mirrors. An old panic stirred Jean Calmet. What other tragedy to be lived through without his father? He remembered that night's strange quarter-hour: he had imagined the Cat Girl slipping a bottle of milk into his pyjamas and warming it between his legs. He himself had taken hold of his penis in his right hand, the sweetness had spurted without his hurrying. Avenging father, get away! I didn't even think about you. Now Thérèse sets the green water of her gaze on you, the copper in a blazing circle deep in her pupil, and suddenly, the odour of the starched handkerchief under the pillow in Lutry came back to him, suddenly the red face on the wall surged back, the hard eyes burned, but it is a joyous odour, these are happy tortures, these nasty deeds which try to strike you at the core and which only succeed in making you taste even purer happiness. The Cat Girl *knew*, Jean Calmet was sure of it, but he felt it like glory. One of Thérèse's rings gleamed in the sun. An iron ring encircling a stone like a bloody berry.

"Did you sleep well?" asked the Cat Girl.

Jean Calmet blushed violently. It was starting again. No, he had to be happy. The corridors of blue ran in his veins. A scream rent the rocks behind the vision.

"How do you sleep?" the Cat Girl went on to ask. "On which side? Do you put your arms under the quilt?"

She added in a dreamy voice:

"I'd like to see you sleeping, Jean." She repeated dreamily: "See you sleeping. See you sleeping. Maybe it's a whim. Still, since we've known each other…"

Jean Calmet was thinking about the enchantress in *The Golden Ass*. Was he going to be metamorphosed, too, into a quadruped to be tortured? He had reread the text that very morning, in one of his classes. The stable where the blows rain on Lucius. Was he going to be changed into an animal by this golden-tressed sorceress? And why not? With pleasure, he imagined himself in the fairy's power. The Pamphile of the tale. And Circe. And Morgan. All the mediatresses of the gloom. And you, white and yellow coat, and you, petal face, face of transparent garden, of Alpine night? Who is calling from the back of the walls? What owl, what panic-stricken animal in the moonlight began to cry in the turbulent fibre? Jean Calmet sees the circles, the copper stria light up in the Cat Girl's eyes. But does she screw? he wondered. Who plunders her little basket? He, who has only had whores, wretched leavings, imagines the Cat Girl's shadowy slit, the tender, honeyed furrow that he has only touched on the shopworn, the weary, and now, for the first time, he slips his hand into Thérèse's panties, he touches the tender, lukewarm lawn, he descends to the hole that emits white resin, he bends over the smooth pelvis, he places his mouth on the curly moss…

The café was full of teenagers who were playing cards and chess. It was exactly ten past five. A few working men in blue smocks were eating sandwiches and drinking beer in the back room, beyond the narrow part of the bar and the toilets. Among the boys and girls who took up almost all of the tables in the main room were many of Jean Calmet's students, those who, just today, had attended the lesson on *The Golden Ass*. It was then that an event took place which has not ceased to echo in the annals of the Gymnase and which the police have placed on the blotter, now that this story is over and that no one on this earth can do anything for Jean Calmet's errant soul. It was ten past five. New teenagers pushed open the door of the Café de l'Évêché, joined the groups of players by sliding over the benches along the walls.

All of a sudden, Jean Calmet screamed. It was a series of violent cries, a series of furious yelps, uninterrupted barking that instantly froze everyone present. He stood up at his table, his arms outstretched; he did not utter anything; he screamed. Then the hideous concert changed into a frantic speech:

"I'm not a dirty bastard," raged Jean Calmet, gesticulating. "I'm clean, I'm not a bastard, leave me alone, all of you, I haven't done anything to you, I'm clean, I'm innocent, I have nothing else to tell you, I'm innocent, I'm innocent!" And he fell flat across the table, breaking glasses of beer and cups, cutting himself on the chin and cheek; suddenly inert, exhausted, as if struck by sacred lightning.

After Jean Calmet's first cries, silence had reigned in the Café de l'Évêché, and all the amazed faces were turned towards him, horrified, full of pity and sadness. Then, as the madman belched forth, cards and dice fell from hands, the waitress and the buffet waiter froze on the spot; an elderly man who was opening the door and innocently entering the café stopped abruptly, his foot in mid-air, his hat held out before him, and he remained standing, petrified, comic in the middle of that amazing scene.

At Jean Calmet's first cries, the Cat Girl had stared at him intensely, her eyes lifted towards him, and she smiled. She smiled with tenderness and admiration. She smiled amid the horror and scandal. Then she placed a hand on the brow of the prostrated man who was crucified on the table strewn with broken glasses, overturned cups. The waitress and the buffet waiter started up again. The old man worked his way up to the nearest chair. The playing cards resumed their places in the moist hands of forty teenagers. Pawns began to move again on seven chessboards. Hands were carried to throats, rubbing them, feeling them as one might after a shipwreck, when reassuring oneself and trying oneself out again in the fresh air full of birds after the horrible onslaught of the sea. Balls of saliva were sent to the bottom of many an unknotting stomach. Tendons unwound. Fingers grew red as though reborn.

It was then that the terrible scales of good and evil called Jean Calmet to appear in their pans. At first, raising his eyes from the horizon of shattered glass where he was bleeding, he saw a whole assembly of young censors who were staring at him. Lenses of eyeglasses gleamed over formidable prophets' beards. Hair of Pharisees brushed over shoulders, and the court stared at him, weighed him, gauged him; they were going to pronounce the sentence, the judges, they were going to speak words that would never cease to echo in Jean Calmet's troubled skull. The terrible words of the father! For that was the result of the scene: the young people had changed into so many avenging fathers, and, deeper still, in the darkness of his memory and heart, it was his father himself, the doctor, the tyrant, that the scandal had brought back to life after several weeks of calm and lightness. As if Jean Calmet had begun screaming in order to bring his father out of the shadows where those five weeks had confined him. As if he had suddenly felt unbearably guilty about this relegation, as if he had killed his father a second time by forgetting him, by driving him out of his days and his dreams, by refusing him access to the Gymnase and to the Cat Girl, by driving him into the red night of the crematorium for ever, into the cold, congealed belly of the urn. But the doctor had avenged himself, he had broken the padlock, smashed the iron bars, he had got out of the columbarium, and his fleshy ghost, his lumbering footfall, his shining red skin, and his hat, his big coat, his hard eyes, his cigar, his smell of wine, his bossy voice, his persecutor's manias, his cries, his contempt, his anger swept down on his son like a tornado! Crushed, Jean Calmet looked at his judge looming massively over the court of his students. The trickle of blood that ran over his chin tickled him like a vile kiss, but he did not dare bring his hand up to the cut, or stand up, or go away.

All that had lasted forty-five seconds.

Already, the waitress was carrying the debris of glass away on a tray, the buffet waiter was changing the sodden table-cloth, the conversations were resuming, the Cat Girl had taken a tissue from her little round basket and was cleaning the blood from Jean Calmet's cheek and chin. Already the faces of the bearded youths, already the long hair of the girls were coming back into their nice sharpness before the bay window; already the evening sun was turning pink; the rooftops, the bridge, the cathedral were beginning to burn against the hill. The Cat Girl opened her little purse and tranquilly lined up her coins on the table. She rose, Jean Calmet rose too; they crossed the café, they opened the door, they were on the Rue de l'Université. Just like yesterday. Just like before. They went up to the little room. They sat down on the gilded bed, they drank coffee in the dolls' cups. Now, for the first time, they lay down side by side under the poster, silent, breathing softly; time envelops them like a fur coat, the light is orange; through the closed windowpane they hear the bells of the cathedral strike six o'clock, and long after they have been stilled, it seems that their echo resounds in the deep stones, the corridors, the courtyards, the gardens and the crypts of the old town. In the room there is a bed; on the bed there are two recumbent figures, a young man with his chin scarred by a long gash, and a girl with a head of luminous hair. They are motionless. They listen to their breathing. A quarter of an hour goes by. The light has grown dim in the room: pink, then grey-pink, then grey, like fire growing pale in the embers and dying out, melting like rays in that calm air.

"I'm cold," says Jean Calmet, and he raises the bedspread, he slides into the sheets, he pulls the woollen blanket up over his shoulders.

The Cat Girl slips in next to him. Warmth settles in. Jean Calmet is motionless, Thérèse is motionless, the blanket encloses them, weighs down maternally, hides them from the world, brings them together. They know it and they do not move. They have closed their eyes. Jean Calmet does not struggle against the sluggishness. A torpor sets in under his brow. Has he slept for a few minutes? Or made himself believe that he is asleep? He is about to lose consciousness when a cool hand is placed on his throat; two fingers follow the cut that burns and a third finger touches his cheek, presses a little; Jean Calmet turns his head, his face is close to the face of Thérèse, who has raised herself up on one elbow and who bends her head and who places on his mouth her moist mouth whose lips move, and Jean Calmet is sucked into that sweetness, he drinks at the deep spring! He breathes an odour of cinnamon, pollen, hot flint... For an instant, it is as though he were finally living his truest childhood, days and days suspended in the green water of dreams. Fresh strength rose in him, and on his lips, in his mouth, the Cat Girl's little tongue ran and was everywhere at once. He did not return her kisses, transported by her: he gave himself up, he let himself float in infantile delight, protected, where all fear had given way. And still this perfume of flowers, of tepid stone, of green, earthy gardens, that smell of childhood, holidays, Easter vacations when the church bells ring. Happy clouds went by in his thoughts: his eyes closed, he saw a verdant prairie, at the back of the landscape a forest scalloped the sky, and little wisps of vapour like sheep drifted over the emerald and blue. The Cat Girl's quick tongue ran over his teeth. Jean Calmet opened his jaws, the tongue insinuated itself deep inside his mouth, it came back, followed the whole contour of his lips, came back to hone itself on the ridge of his teeth. The Cat Girl lay down against him; he breathed her warm, tart smell near her ear, where she must have washed herself with eau de cologne that morning, and the odour of her hair, riper, more hidden, like a secret that she had exposed for a moment before shutting it up again in her golden tresses.

It was growing dark.

The lights of the Gymnase illuminated the walls above the recumbent figures, and Jean Calmet marvelled at the distance that separated him, at that moment, from the classrooms where he would give his lessons on the following morning.

Suddenly the Cat Girl knelt close to him; she quickly unbuttoned Jean Calmet's shirt, spreading the cloth over his armpits and plunged to the centre of his chest where she placed a kiss. Her hair caressed the throat, the collarbones of Jean Calmet. The spots of light on the wall disappeared, the night was complete, but the Cat Girl's form and hair filled it with sparks and rockets, and Jean Calmet marvelled at the fact that the darkness was so scintillating and tender in its simplicity.

Then the Cat Girl gently licked his chest.

Then, while her tongue lapped his nipples and a cool hand was descending over his navel, Jean Calmet felt the extraordinary violence of the sensations and visions that carried him away the way that typhoons rip away whole houses, beginning by shaking them, then breaking them, tearing them asunder, sucking them up, hurling them, scattering all their components violently into the air like castles that have exploded.

All his castles exploded.

He was shattered and he was flying.

A terrible coolness streamed into his bones, riddled his veins with white droplets, unknotted his throat, ran between his shoulders. The Cat Girl's hand touched his navel. Two fingers slipped into the garment, they ran along his pubis, made a stop, resumed their gentle way, climbed back around his pelvis, came back to massage his loins gently.

Jean Calmet was motionless, and he wanted to stay that way. Lying in the dark, flat on his back, his arms resting alongside his body, his belly bare, his legs spread. A corpse, yes, I'm dead, I'm made of stone, I've been laid to rest for ever on my own grave and I have only to clasp my hands over my chest to be really changed into cold limestone or marble!

He joined his hands, the fingers raised towards the sky, he closed his eyes in the darkness and recalled the strange Sire François who lies in the same position, at the bottom of Château Jacquemart de la Sarraz. Outside, the castle raises its towers above the vale of wolves and witches. In the shadow of the chapel the cruel Sire sleeps in the stone under the sorrowful vigil of his widow, his daughter and his two sons, who have prayed unceasingly for six centuries for the remission of their master's sins. What struck Jean Calmet, the first time he went into the Jacquemart with his father, was the fact that the sculptor had covered the recumbent man with repugnant, slithering creatures: snakes squeezed his chest and arms. Toads buried themselves in his eyes, ran over his cheeks. Thus the bad spirits of the Venoge had come out of the cold river and the night of the ponds, they had joined their suzerain that they covered for eternity with their scales and their drool.

But a tepid mouth is running over Jean Calmet, two smooth, warm hands feel his ribs and his back. He is not guilty like the abominable Sire of la Sarraz! I haven't killed anyone. I'm good. The sorry Sire François robbed wayfarers, raped them, tortured them, killed them for his pleasure. Fire, blood, black vengeance. I'm innocent and I'm new. The dead man has the kiss of ghouls. A child's tongue plays over my breast. O deep night. Mystery of sharing and the denial of all sharing. O night of privilege. Mercy.

Kneeling, the Cat Girl seized Jean Calmet's wrists and secured them, by the pressure of her hands, on the flat of the sheet. Crucified now, he felt the strain on his arms with strange pleasure. He was breathing slowly, his sides rose. In the darkness, he saw his armpits offered up to Thérèse's kisses, his smooth belly, his hips quivering under her caress. With a gentle hand, she assured herself that Jean Calmet was still crucified. Then she seized the buckle of his belt, unfastened it rapidly, opened the fly of his trousers which she drew off, then his shorts, and, like little parachutes, she let them drop on the rug. Jean Calmet was naked under her alert hands. Cat Girl, braced, a succubus, an exquisite vampire, bent now over his penis. Her hair caressed Jean Calmet's thighs: her mouth, rapid, placed – on his knees – brief salutations, like the calling cards brought to the table of a host at a marriage, a funeral, from which one withdraws on tiptoe, leaving him without witness to his joy or sorrow, and, in the street, turns back to look at the windows of the apartment lit as one would on the only paradise in which one might have been able to live, cherished at last. But the succubus did not leave, and with its muzzle, with its sweet snout, with its maw, it grazed Jean Calmet's penis, which straightened up without impatience towards the demon's happy breath.

He began to gasp quietly under her lips.

Now the Cat Girl shed her clothes with nimble speed in the darkness where Jean Calmet sensed her every movement. On Jean's chest lay the round breasts, then the sweet-haired head lodged itself against his throat, the belly glued itself to his, the pelvis moulded itself to his pelvis, the Cat Girl's long thighs pressed his, and her curly pubis crushed itself against Jean Calmet's penis, which burned gently and took on its form under the round, constant pressure. The Cat Girl rose slightly, she panted in her turn, the tip of Jean Calmet's penis seated itself in the pubic hair of the succubus, who moved her croup to fit it deeper in her antrum. Everything was all right. The promise of Dionysus had been fulfilled. Jean Calmet felt himself sliding into the milky path towards the maternal cave. He exulted.

Suddenly the power failed.

Panic swooped down on him.

He was cold, he was being drawn down into space, he was terribly alone on a rock that was drifting in the open sea, he did not know who was calling him from the top of a tower and who he could never reach, he was condemned by a court of ghostly ancestors; deep in his bones, a burned wolf, an exiled prince, a snake trampled and despised, he howled as no man on earth will ever again howl.

Shame crowned him with iron.

His penis fell back against his belly.

He himself remained motionless.

The Cat Girl moved a little more. Jean Calmet knew that she was pretending not to know: speechless, he closed himself off, he sealed himself up ludicrously while, with all his senses, he waited for the word that would unbind him, comfort him, bring him back from the dead. The Cat Girl did the irreparable: with one finger she grazed Jean Calmet's penis. The doctor thundered in the dazzling clouds, flung himself into her, took her, left her panting and gluey, took her again, broke her, illuminated her, filled her, flooded her. The doctor bursting with laughter.

"So, you've been humiliated, my son. Didn't you take your vitamins? You've gone limp? Look at your old father. Wrinkled, burned, but he still makes the women dance on his cock. This woman, too, you miserable sap. Your Cat Girl. Yes, *yours*. When a man isn't up to screwing his conquests, he should skip the bluffing!"

That is what his father bellowed into Jean Calmet's anguish-filled ears. Into his end-of-the-world ears.

The Cat Girl lay back down against him where he was still motionless; she pressed her lips against his temple and remained quiet in the darkness. A few minutes went by.

"Do you want to sleep here?" she asked a little later.

"No," Jean Calmet said simply.

He found his clothes in the dark, dressed quickly, placed his hand – by way of farewell – on the brow of the Cat Girl, who had not stirred from her bed. Then he went out into the cold night.

Crossing the Rue de la Cité, he raised his eyes towards the little room that he had just left, and he was torn by what he saw, completely filling his wound with tender, violent-tempered nostalgia: on the window sill stood a bottle of milk like a first childhood image. When he got into his car, tears were running down his face.

Isabelle died on Easter Monday; it was 23 April, she had held out longer than expected, she was exhausted, she remained lying down, only getting up for a moment to greet the school friends who met in her room every day.

She was buried in Crécy.

There was an immense crowd of boys and girls in blue jeans, a line of farmers in black, holding their hats in their hands.

Jean Calmet was not at the funeral.

They told him those things the next day, it was just when school reopened, a little breeze was blowing over La Cité, the sky burned blue, groups of children called to one another and broke up on the pavements of La Mercerie.

Jean Calmet was dying of shame. He had abandoned Isabelle. He had gone to see her only once, on her birthday, 20 March, her friends had eaten cake, they had opened bottles of wine, listened to Leonard Cohen, and Joan Baez, and Donovan, and Bob Dylan.

As long as he lived, Jean Calmet would reproach himself for not going to the funeral. Why had he taken sleeping pills that morning, knocking himself out, going back to sleep with his head tucked under a heavy pillow, waking up at five o'clock in the afternoon, just when they were serving the buffet at the farm in Crécy? He had not dared appear before the eyes of Isabelle's parents, her family, all of his students gathered there. He was in fear. An evil, shameful fear that had ensnared him from the moment he had learnt of his student's death, a vile dread of being reproached for living, he, the useless one, the bachelor, the restless one, while the beautiful girl had been covered with earth. "What are you doing here, Monsieur Calmet? Are you crying? And are you enjoying the tingling of the sun on your skin? You'd do better to take our daughter's place, my friend. For what use you're making of your life… And then, you'd be doing us a favour. When I stop and think that, at thirty-nine, all you're good for is distilling the affectations of a few decadent poets. What a shame, Monsieur Calmet. You hesitate? Look at our daughter once more, let's seal the casket, let's throw her into the hole, and we'll go and drink a glass of wine at our grandparents' farm. There'll be sweet wafers, cakes. Just what you need to drug your cowardice, right, Monsieur Calmet, Monsieur the distinguished Latin master at the Gymnase!"

Jean Calmet looked at the photos of the funeral. With infinite sorrow, he had them tell him about the afternoon.

There, it is over. The class remembers the little dead girl. Jean Calmet sees the Cat Girl almost every day. Often one of his students brings him a poem, a song, and it is always the same title, which scalds him with chagrin and distress as soon as he opens the envelope: *For Isabelle*.

Some evenings, the summer already hangs in the branches of the lime trees.

One afternoon late in April, when the weather was mild, Jean Calmet followed a cat on the path at the edge of the lake. That cat spoke to him of many things:

"You don't understand anything," said the cat. "You're an ass, Jean Calmet, an idiot who's drifting from bad to worse. I'm fond of you, Jean Calmet, you've got loads of good points, but why don't you stop acting like a fool day after day?"

At that time, Jean Calmet was walking tranquilly behind the oracle; he listened to him with obvious interest.

"Look at me," said the cat. "Do you see me worrying? Do I stew in remorse or sadness?"

101

"You don't have a father," said Jean Calmet, who kicked a white pebble on the path.

"Nothing doing," said the cat. And he raised his tail towards the cloudless sky; one could see his pink anus in his black behind.

Jean Calmet felt good. All along the little path stood hedges and tepid walls; on the right, and on the left, the lake that was beginning to grow red in the twilight.

"It's beautiful," the cat went on to say. "Fill your eyes, fill your fibre, cram your soul, Jean Calmet. One fine morning you won't be here any more to enjoy your ecstasies of the living. See that boat, in front of Évian? Look at that white, that nougat bar against the green and red. And Savoy – see it? Blue and purple, all the mountains resound with cascades and rock slides into chasms. And those mists – over near the Rhône? Do you remember the ponds full of eggs, the snakes that zigzagged over the still water where the red rays were reflected? Remember the kites over the mouth of the river? And the young fish in the bubbles?"

"And you, cat," said Jean Calmet, "do you remember your father's face?"

He regretted his question at once, for the cat turned around and looked at him in amusement.

But they continued to go on their way. For a moment, neither of them spoke. The sun is an orange. The lake is covered with bands of gold.

The cat is first to break the silence.

"Jean Calmet!"

"Yes! That's me," said Jean Calmet.

"Have you thought about your death yet, Jean Calmet? Don't answer. I'm not talking about the death of others. Nor of its echo in your skull. Nor of your dear cemeteries. I'm talking about your death, Jean Calmet. Have you thought about your nothingness yet?"

"Cat not be happy," said Jean Calmet. "Mean cat ask companion too sad question. Companion not understand why cat mean on such a walk."

"Don't act like a fool," said the cat. "Answer about your death. You're keeping quiet, aren't you? You don't understand anything, Jean Calmet. You're half-alive. You're eating yourself up. You're more ash than your father. And your blood? Your flesh that's still young? Your head full of foolishness? You're kidding, Jean Calmet. It's the spirit of Dionysus or nothing. Pan or death. Salvation through one's works or the last ravine at the bottom of the last hole in the last mountain in Greece or elsewhere. Go to the end of the oldest mythologies or into each hour's brazier. You're all washed up, Jean Calmet, unless you make up your mind!"

Undulating, the cat walked over the pebbles of the path, his fur glossy, his paws precise. Jean Calmet admired the animal's exasperating sureness and could not listen to what he had to tell him. The cat was right. Perfectly. He was stewing in boredom, he was sinking into it. When would he get out of the brambles? If his father saw him following this prophet... What a burst of laughter! Ah, bollocks to my lousy father. And immediately the vision of the red bruiser revolted him to the depths of his being. Horror seized him. He looked at the beautiful, lithe cat, saw his power, saw his wiliness, saw his pleasure on that path, and decided to listen to him. To obey him methodically. He had to be happy now. He had to flee from the ravines and lethal space where he had taken an unwholesome pleasure for years. Nothing was going to stop him.

Then, because he understood his agreement, the cat knew that Jean Calmet no longer needed him. He took a fork to the right, started along a trail that climbed towards an ivy-covered house, slipped into a hedge and disappeared.

Marvelling at the encounter, Jean Calmet transformed the animal's elegance into supernatural beauty, his careful tread into mysterious adventure and his words into divine warning. He recalled his arrival at Ouchy, the delicacy of the quays, the old hotels, pink in the evening light, the pavement cafés overflowing with young people. He remembered the hours that he had spent after the crematorium and the funeral buffet. He felt anew the joy that he had known then, and afterwards, his gloom. And what have I done since? he wondered. And what of my scene at the Café de l'Évêché? And the little room on the Rue de la Cité-Devant? And he hardened his resolve to be good, to be happy, to live in glad strength and faith.

In the weeks that followed, the Cat Girl was particularly good and gentle, and Jean Calmet spent several nights with her. He squeezed himself against the wall, under the poster of the panther. Thérèse kissed him, took him in her, kept him, took him again for hours. Now Jean Calmet loved her, he was really her lover, she said that she was happy, and he was happy too, that beginning of May, when the birds of La Cité woke them up at dawn in tender happiness.

Around that time, Jean Calmet was called in to see the principal of the Gymnase. Colonel, member of government, Monsieur Grapp was a tall, righteous man, with physical strength apparent in his powerful, nervous movements. He was bald, with an enormous, dented skull. He always wore dark glasses.

Jean Calmet hated this summons. What did Grapp want of him? He knew his violent rages, his prejudices of the so-called honest man faced with unexpected events. Most of all, he feared in him the senior, the master. He had yet to meet him, or even to spy him from afar in one of the little streets of La Cité, without experiencing a sense of fear, of uneasiness, of remorse as well, very abrupt, sharp, as if he had been found at fault suddenly and all his ruses exposed. What have I done this time? thought Jean Calmet at those encounters. What is he going to take me to task for? And he would run away as fast as his legs could carry him in the other direction, or duck into a corridor, from which he would watch Grapp go by: his nose glued to the chicken-wired glass, sweating with anguish and ashamed, how many times he had watched the bald man move forward with great strides, vigorous, a fighter, while he, Jean Calmet, burrows into the dusty shadows of the corridor!

Several times, in the teachers' room or in the vestibule leading to the principal's office, Jean Calmet felt the same agitation, the same fear that he had experienced when going to his father's consultation room. He spies Grapp's tall frame, his caramel-custard camel's-hair coat, his dark glasses, the double crêpe soles, and he immediately finds himself trembling and humiliated as at Les Peupliers, when he used to knock at the doctor's door, sweating with rage and anguish. Dozens of times he wondered if his fellow schoolmasters also went through that fear. Did François Clerc and Verret flee when the bald giant loomed up? He observed them from a corner of the teachers' room, where he pretended to look up a telephone number or consult a dictionary. No answer. François Clerc and Verret looked relaxed, both of them, and conversed calmly with Grapp. But perhaps they were feigning ease? Perhaps they were hideously uneasy, as he was, at seeing themselves transfixed by the Master. He would ask François the question one of these days. If he dares. For did this blunt question not mean revealing oneself to the core?

He reported at the secretary's office, and Madame Oisel, whose green eyes and comely bosom Jean Calmet admired, asked him to wait a few minutes until Monsieur principal was free. Jean Calmet, who was becoming sweaty, fastened on to the spectacle of Madame Oisel. She had gone back to her typewriter, and her breasts were trembling in her thin blouse. Twenty-five years old, tanned, happy. But she also intimidated him by having access to the principal at all times, by being tied to the master's humours, to his plans, to his secrets. She took part in the Eleusinian mysteries: admitted to the tripod, to the embers, to the philtres, and in the smoke of the god-principal-of-men, she exhales an initiatory power that pulverizes Jean Calmet. She is a beautiful woman. She is happy. She has found *her* master: a handsome, sophisticated man, a Frenchman, a trainee at the school who teaches maths and physical education.

So Jean Calmet was waiting for the principal to open the temple door to him. He sweated more profusely now, wiped his hands on his trousers, fearing that as a result of rubbing his palms over his knees and thighs he would leave obscene, comical yellow spots. Madame Oisel ripped a letter from her typewriter, applied the seal of the Gymnase to it, signed it, folded it, slid it into its envelope, licked the flap with a long tongue, pressed it quickly with her fist and threw it into a small cardboard box where the god's mail was piled. The principal's door opened, and Monsieur Grapp appeared on its threshold. Jean Calmet wanted to rise; something in him went mad, refused, shut itself up in a black burrow; suddenly the resistance gave way, he got to his feet with apparent ease, he moved forward smiling at Monsieur Grapp. Enormous, fantastic, the tall figure was framed in the doorway like an immense yellow, woollen parallelepiped. The dark glasses crowned the camel's-hair sinisterly, and, above them, his bald skull gleamed, white, dented. The giant opened his mouth, saliva welled up at the corners, his uneven teeth appeared like tombstones at the back of an old graveyard for child-eaters. And his hairy hand reaches out, enormous, towards Jean Calmet... Jean Calmet, who stumbles over the doorstep, blushes, feels sweat squirting from the root of every hair on his head, stretches out in turn his moist hand, follows the glutton into his lair, drops into the thin armchair that the suzerain designates. Imposing, the suzerain is comfortably ensconced behind his desk, big-boned, massive, his dark glasses hiding and revealing glaucous globes that go through Jean Calmet's heart.

"I won't beat around the bush, Monsieur Calmet," said the Director in a loud voice, and Jean Calmet noticed once again his Vaud accent, in which the humming and the thickness of the *sh* had retained their peasant flavour. "You're well liked in this school, Monsieur Calmet, we respect the high level of your professional conscientiousness. Your students work, you know how to make them enthusiastic, I know through many parents that you are respected and admired. That's why I feel free to speak to you very firmly today."

He struck a pose, grinned; Jean Calmet prepared himself to be knocked out and devoured.

"I didn't want to speak to you about it right away, Monsieur Calmet. You needed to get hold of yourself and think things over. I'm talking about the incident at the Café de l'Évêché. Naturally, the whole business came to my attention. Several colleagues spoke to me about it, and some parents let me know how astonished they were. Let me add that I got a discreet call from the criminal-investigation department wanting to know if drugs had been involved. We're very much in the public eye in our trade, Monsieur Calmet, and that makes it all the harder for me to understand how you, with the keen sense of the duty that binds us all, could let yourself go in such an extreme way. What happened, Monsieur Calmet? Had you been drinking? Did you lose your head completely? An entirely understandable moment of confusion, provided that it stops there. Tell me, Monsieur Calmet. After all, I could be your father..."

Jean Calmet made a terrible effort at staring into the mysterious glasses: he could not speak; his hand, damp with sweat, was trembling on the armrest of the chair.

"I was taken ill," he said at last.

Monsieur Grapp nodded approvingly, as he might have encouraged a child.

"I lost control of myself," Jean Calmet continued in a weak voice. "I said incoherent things… I couldn't see anything…"

"The trouble is that you screamed those things," the Director broke in harshly. "In your position it's most unfortunate. There were more than thirty students in that café… but that's another question I'll take up in due course. But you acknowledge, Monsieur Calmet, that your behaviour was perfectly scandalous."

Jean Calmet admitted it, mumbling.

"Do you have a problem with your nerves, Monsieur Calmet? Shouldn't you seek help, have yourself treated in a clinic for a few weeks?"

Jean Calmet gave a start, horrified. The clinic, the psychiatrists, his poor heart drilled right through, the cell, the diet… He dared to state that he was in good health.

"Do you drink, Monsieur Calmet? People have often seen you sitting at students' tables, with beer, aperitifs…"

No, Jean Calmet did not drink. To be sure, he liked the company of young people. No, he did not encourage them to drink. No, no, Monsieur, he did not have any special taste for alcohol. No, wine was not necessary to him. And it never had been.

"You ought to get married, Monsieur Calmet," said the Director. "It's no good for a man to be alone. Especially you, who come from a large family – you must feel even lonelier now. I knew your dear father, you know; now there's a man who lived for his family, surrounded by children, by patients! Ah, what a fine man he was. We don't have enough people like that nowadays. This country is in real need of them. His greatness, Monsieur Calmet! His energy! His strength! His devotion! In a word —" He broke off suddenly. "I'm counting on you not to allow the little incident in the Café de l'Évêché to happen again. Think of your family, think of us. Give yourself a breath of air. Find a young lady, give her children, Monsieur Calmet. *Et libri, et liberi*, as your dear Latins said. You'd have time to keep your nose in a book and raise a little family. All right, good day, Monsieur Calmet. It's been a pleasure to see you. I have complete confidence in you."

He rose; his overwhelming figure in the yellow jacket hid the whole window, a big hairy hand reached out towards Jean Calmet, crushed his, shook it in mid-air between the cannibal's belly and the tentatively spared victim. The survivor found himself completely bewildered in the corridor, where the bronze Ramuz stared at him with its vacant, nauseating orbs.

Jean Calmet went down to the Place de la Palud. He was not thinking, he walked mechanically, it was the end of the afternoon, a bit tepid, a bit sugary. He knew where he was going. He was not ashamed. He had to drive away the scene that he had just experienced with another uncommon scene. He had to escape Grapp's bulk blocking the window, killing life.

Tranquilly, Jean Calmet walked down the Place de la Palud to the Place de la Louve. He pushed open a door with his right hand, started up a staircase. Fourth floor. A black-painted wooden door. A card is stuck against it: Pernette Colomb. Jean Calmet rings. The door opens: Pernette Colomb. Her big breasts in the open bodice. Her eye lengthened with glossy makeup. Fifty-eight years old. Plump, her mouth red, a vile, ironic face.

She fusses, places a kiss on Jean Calmet's cheek, makes a curtsey and, with a comical gesture, invites him into her three-room apartment.

"How's our little professor? It's been a while since he's been back to see his Pernette! He must have had lots of things to do and lady friends to love!"

Jean Calmet is not put off: under the banter, he spots a kind of veiled affection that gently drives away his anguish: Pernette slides next to him on the couch:

"We want to think about the little present first, right, sweetie? That way, we'll have our minds clear for what comes afterwards. The usual, little prof?"

Without looking at her, into the hand that she has placed on his thigh, Jean Calmet slips the single fifty-franc note that he had ready in his pocket. Pernette snatches it and tosses it into the drawer of a chest, which she double locks. She claps her hands, comes running back towards Jean and flings herself against him on the couch, raising aloft her bare legs that gleam. She puts her arms around him; her red mouth that smells of grenadine settles quickly on his mouth.

"Come, baby."

She pulls him by the arms. She pushes him into the other room, stops him in front of a sink. The water is warm. She unbuckles his belt, slips her hand into his briefs, grasps Jean Calmet's penis, lays it on the cold rim of the basin. A bar of pink soap. Two hands, under the hot stream, slowly wash his erect penis. He holds his trousers up over his thighs. He follows the fat woman to the flat bed. Slip. Pink girdle. Legs already bare. She bends over the panting belly, the grenadine mouth sucks, licks, a hand comes and goes under Jean Calmet's narrow back with surprising speed.

The black panties slide over heavy thighs. Pubis almost rose-pink. The hand of the master of Latin language and literature at Gymnase Cantonal de la Cité searches in the pubic nest, spreads lips lubricated with Vaseline.

"Come on! Come on!" Sighs. Squirms. Jean Calmet kneeling in the rotundities, the cannonballs, the casks, the smooth hams of Pernette Colomb. Once she explained that name "Pernette" to him. "Actually, my name is Denise. But my father was crazy about me. He was a drinker, my father was.

He was a roofer. That was in Fribourg, before the war. He used to take me on his bike. We used to ride all around the countryside. We stopped at cafés. He would drink apple brandies, absinthes, one after the other, they had real absinthe in those days. My father called me his ladybird, his *pernette*, he used to laugh and tell his friends that I was his only love, his consolation and his grace. One day when he'd had more to drink than usual, he fell from a roof and split his head open on the pavement. Since then I've never wanted people to call me anything but Pernette. That's all I've got left of him. My pen name, professor!" Jean Calmet buried himself in the fat coccinella who could feign emotion adeptly. "*Chéri! Chéri!*" cries the bug. *Français, encore un effort,* thinks *le chéri,* whom the word injures. But the wet sweetness presses him, sucks him; he anchors himself deep within her, almost motionless, he spills out into the happy cave.

As he leaves, Jean Calmet is not sad, and the clamour from the square promises to keep him warm in a little while. Denise has some nice words: as she has known her client for years, she offers him a glass of liqueur brandy so that he does not go out into the city too lonely.

Jean Calmet receives another grenadine-flavoured kiss. He hesitates in the doorway. He goes out. Yes, of course, I'll come back. It is in the corridor that the sadness descends on him. He goes down the stairs. Out on the square again, he feels a shame that chills him, makes him flee the eyes of the people. Oh Jean Calmet, you know all too well that Denise is the feminine of Dionysus! The sister, the daughter, the exalted companion of the divine! Derision. Parody. But night is falling. Jean Calmet lowers his head, and, at that very moment, as one gives in to its panels of darkness, he consents to turn away from the great mountains full of gods.

Part III
Jealousy

His bones are full of the sin of his youth...

Job 20:11

D URING THAT TIME, a demonstration was held at the
Gymnase, one which had everybody in the region talking and gave Monsieur Grapp lasting fame. For different
reasons, the demonstration was to change Jean Calmet's life.

It had all started at the cathedral, during the graduation
ceremony, which marks the promotion of hundreds of boys
and girls from secondary school to the Gymnase. While in
the very solemn pulpit to recite a poem, a student seized
the opportunity to criticize the system roundly, to question
the curriculum, make fun of his teachers and persuade his
classmates not to stand for any more.

Frightful scandal.

At the graduation, and in the hallowed pulpit of the cathedral, a radical student, a leftist, had insulted the authorities! As the newspapers played up the incident, the whole
region reacted: the countryside jumped at the chance to
criticize a school that turns out nothing but leftists all year
long, the cities were divided equally between the pseudo
hard-liners of the right and jokers with socialist tendencies,
parents wrote vengeful letters to the editors and fought to
have their sons' hair cut.

Monsieur Grapp and the Board of Education made a
spectacular decision: the speech-maker was suspended,
so that instead of coming to school in April, he would not
return to the Gymnase until September. This provided
the excuse, at the end of April, for all sorts of goings-on,

115

which the left-wing groups stirred up ceaselessly: parades with cloth and cardboard signs, impromptu gatherings on the little squares of La Cité, daily flyers from *La Taupe*, *Spartacus*, *La Ligue Marxiste* or *Rupture*, speeches by the suspended youth before the Board of Education. Let Pierre Zwahlen back in, was the slogan they chanted on the Place de la Barre; mingling with the happy, colourful crowd were lots of tramps, drunkards and phoney legionnaires, denizens of the quarter and its two broken-down cafés. It was on a fine spring afternoon, the leaves crowned the little trees of the Place de la Barre with a light fuzz and the great chestnut tree looked one hundred years younger. Gesticulating and laughing, the young people had come out of the Rue de l'Université in a disorderly procession where they danced, where they sang. Girls had flowers in their hair, pansies stuck in their braids, little roses; others brandished bouquets of tulips that they had picked in the public parks, in Ouchy, in Montbenon, since it all belongs to everyone! The flowers are ours, the festival is ours. Nothing was missing. Cheerful placards: "Make love", "Bawl out your teachers", "Change the school", "Your parents are morons" and "Love again", "Freedom", as in a poem by Éluard. Long dresses, bare feet, jeans, all the uniforms left at the river's edge by the Confederates at the end of that fateful day of 6 April 1865, and then pretty songs again, 'Le Partisan', 'L'Internationale', 'Bandiera rossa', 'Le Temps des cerises', and dumbfounded people on the pavements, the local alcoholics whose three-day beards are like thistles, old prostitutes delighted by all that clamour, three drunken chimney sweeps who throw their top hats into the air, a nasty grocer who wanted to call the cops but who winds up singing 'Le Temps des cerises' with the others, a midget projected like a cannonball from the Café du Pavement, he has a hard time stopping, he crashes into a group of flowered girls, squeezes himself against them, stretches his outsized arms, clutches a long orange skirt, seizes a waist in both hands and starts to go round and round, dances, spins with the beautiful, the tall, the sublime adolescent of all his dreams.

Jean Calmet watched the spectacle with intense pleasure. He was sitting on the little wall that bounds the car park of the police barracks, at the foot of the Chatêau, he liked the colour of the sky, that intense blue against the farandole, he was having fun listening to the slogans repeated through the megaphone, the milling of the crowd, the clamour, and when Zwahlen gave his speech, he listened to it and was gladdened by it. Suddenly, he became gloomy again, and anguish brought a lump to his throat: he had just noticed, in the middle of a moving group of girls and boys, a little round basket that reminded him pointedly of Red Riding Hood's offering. He stared at the group: the basket appeared between two hips, half-hidden now by canvas and cardboard signs. But all of a sudden Jean Calmet made out a head of golden hair that streamed down from a yellow and white fur hat: Thérèse. And who is holding her hand? That young man with long hair? It is Marc, that melancholy boy Marc, the fiancé of the dead girl of Crécy, Marc-Orpheus with the beautiful hair who had his picture taken on the cold stone slab with the translucent Eurydice at the Gates of Hell. Marc is holding Thérèse's hand. A whirlwind of dresses and ribbons. Shouts. Bursts of laughter. Then the megaphones incite the crowd to gather at the Place du Tunnel and, in a few minutes, the Place de la Barre is deserted, the chants can still be heard, fading into the distance, spring remains master of the field.

Jean Calmet met Thérèse at the Café de l'Évêché: she told him about the demonstration without mentioning Marc. She had started again at the École des Beaux-Arts,

Thérèse; she wanted to be an interior decorator, it's quicker than becoming a teacher. No, she had not gone back to Montreux. She would spend the weekend there. Montreux: Jean Calmet saw the clumps of palm trees before the purple lake, under the battlements of Gothic hotels on the gulf of molten gold.

"Will you come and pick me up Sunday evening?"

"Where will you be?"

"At the Café Apollo, I think. Take a look and see if I'm there. I'm not going to spend the whole day with my mother. Yes, go by the Apollo around six o'clock. We'll have a drink and go back to La Cité. *D'ac?*"

"*D'ac*," said Jean Calmet. She always said *d'ac* for *d'accord*. He began speaking the way she did. "Do any work today?"

No answer. Evasive gesture. Smile wiped off by her tongue, oh cat, cat with the transparent blouse, cat with leather and copper necklaces, with Arab and Afghan rings; cat between whose thighs the hair is like frizzy bronze turnings from which emerge the sweet wings of passion and desire sputtering in the wet darkness.

Then they leave each other, Jean Calmet goes home to mark homework papers, he goes to bed early, he sleeps. In the morning he gets up reminding himself of Sunday's rendezvous in Montreux.

It was eight o'clock when he arrived at the Gymnase. He parked his car at La Mercerie, and, as soon as he got out, he sensed that something strange was happening. Spotting him, a fellow whose face was unknown to him ducked behind a wall. Cardboard signs on sticks were heaped up on the benches of the promenade. Young teenagers – apparently schoolboys or kids in the first year of their vocational apprenticeships – were smoking cigarettes, leaning against the front window of the Café de l'Évêché.

At that little green hour of the dawn when the first male pigeons of the cathedral give their first beak-to-beak kisses to their Ronsardian hen pigeons, Jean Calmet, the nice young teacher, would never have guessed what the morning had in store for him, and the fatal effect which that discovery was to have on his own life, already worn away by a number of onslaughts and moods severe enough to drive him mad.

But it was the time for reading *La Tribune.* Jean Calmet, sipping a tepid *ristretto,* glanced over the newspaper, marvelling at the amount of rubbish that graced its greyish pages.

A second *ristretto* scarcely warmer. Arrival of some hurried students. Cigarette smoke. Cups of Ovaltine. School bell perceptible through the open door.

Suddenly, the carnival.

About a hundred teenagers come running up from the Rue de la Mercerie and sit down in the lower courtyard of the Gymnase; they laugh, they shout slogans. It is a *sit-in*: as on an American college campus, they are seated, they are having lots of fun, the teachers step over them to get into the building. Gesticulating, about fifty boys rush into the upper schoolyard. A megaphone calls on the students of the Gymnase to rebel against the decision of the principal and the Board. Milling of the crowd. Shouts. Groups prepare to enter the Academy building. All of a sudden, there is silence, everyone stands petrified: in the doorway of the Academy, massive, immense, skull shining, his nose fitted with his fearsome dark glasses, Monsieur Grapp appeared, contemplating the adversary, almost dreamily. But despite the concentrated strength that he embodies, there is something else that stupefies the onlookers: in his hand – a new monstrosity, an object emerging from earliest times, an aggressive, dominant symbol, as astonishing as an archaic beast – Grapp holds a whip, a long cannoneer's whip as curly as a snake ready to strike, a long thong of braided leather gushing from a shank gleaming and thick as a truncheon. A moment of amazement, a boy gives a shout, the megaphone takes up his refrain and the crowd of demonstrators marches on the main door. Grapp raises the whip, makes it whistle and springs at the besiegers. Bewildered, the boys fall back. Later on, they will explain why: it is not fear, or respect, it is shock that made them yield. They are confused, flabbergasted, several laugh nervously. Alain and Marc take pictures. But the whip still whistles, Grapp moves forward, all of a sudden the whole group starts running away, reaching the main gate in disorder. Then Grapp no longer restrains himself, he runs from one to the other, the whip on high, he overtakes the fugitives, he bounds up to the wooden barracks at the western entrance, he comes leaping back, the whip still raised, whistling, he goes through the gate, he pursues the survivors into the Rue de la Cité-Devant, he retraces his steps, he seizes the venerable gate, he heaves the iron grille shut. The courtyard is empty. Monsieur Grapp is master of the field.

Jean Calmet saw the whole scene from a window of the teachers' room. He, too, is stupefied. In the days that follow, the students will give him details which he could not catch from the floor above: Monsieur Grapp drooled and foamed at the mouth as he ran, he uttered inarticulate cries, a student caught a whiplash in the eye... Nothing can heighten the panic created by the spectacle of that colossus armed with the hideous, deadly braid. In the days that follow, caricatures, photos, messages will rain in. Grapp will be written about in *Le Monde*: his portrait, armed with the whip, will appear in *Le Canard enchaîné*: glory, and forced laughter, black humour or red humour, once more the people in the region are divided and cursing at one another.

What is a whip? Jean Calmet mused on the instrument and its powers. The whip of the executioner, the whip of the lover, the whip of humiliation and pleasure. Whip up the blood. A whiplash. The whipping post. Whip a disobedient child. You'll get a whipping! A whipping father. And Grapp was immediately nicknamed *le Père Fouettard* by everyone. But in the photos, in the newspapers, the dark glasses, the dented baldness and the rictus sternly rectified anything good-natured that those words might suggest. On the contrary, that nickname, "*Père Fouettard*", had a sadistic air, and the man's stature, his enormous shoulders, his thick neck, his hairy hands gave him tremendous support. Seeing the newspaper pictures that the printer's ink darkened and simplified in a sinister way, even people who had never met Monsieur Grapp sensed his irascible strength, violent-tempered, concentrated, as an almost unbearable fact. Like a kind of obscenity.

One night, Jean Calmet saw the whip in a dream; he cried out, he awoke, angry at his fear and promising himself to keep watch over himself. It was no use: Grapp's size had increased even more since the incident, and the grotesqueness, the buffoonery, the madness of the scene had served only to increase, mysteriously, the irrational, brutal authority that Jean Calmet saw in him. He realized, in the conversations that he had almost every day with his students at the Café de l'Évêché, that they had reacted and were continuing to react exactly as he had: they had been subjected to the whip as a paternal warning willed by destiny. Exasperated, furious, or simply ironic, they had given ground, they had fled under the threat of the terrible thong. But rather than to it and its whistling, gleaming leather, they had yielded to its authoritarian symbol, to the symbol of the Father, to the sceptre of order, and that hierarchic fatality comforted them obscurely, deeply, as much as it annoyed them on the surface. Authority had manifested itself, glorified by its badge of office: all was well. They could go on being children since the Father was in power. Since he was watching. Since he had shown himself in all his stormy, domineering magnificence.

Zeus! Jupiter thundering! Paternal analogies emerged from the depths of the ages. And the lieutenant of the

Creator, the King-God, the father of the State, the prince-father of his subjects, all the hypostases of the paterfamilias, stern and punishing in his rough benevolence.

In class, one of those mornings, *The Golden Ass* was neglected for talk about the event, and Jean Calmet became aware once more of the attention that all of his students had given to it. It was not so much because dozens of posters and piles of handbills bore witness to its impact. It was more serious: like the discovery of the Dependence, and they were curiously relieved and comforted by it.

That morning, from his desk, Jean Calmet was watching Marc particularly – Marc who was fleeing him. Marc is sitting at the back of the classroom, in the corner opposite the windows, next to Sandrine Dudan. They get on well together, Marc and Sandrine, they back each other up, they cheat together, they draw, they make movies. Sandrine is small, dark, quick, a she-goat of the scree slopes. Marc was fleeing him… Something was bothering Jean Calmet: since the first demonstration, Marc had been leaving more and more frequent traces around Thérèse's place: first, it had been a loose-leaf book, a scarf, then his assignment book and, with a kind of provocative audacity, the *Romans grecs et latins de la Pléiade* that Jean Calmet had lent him. From the doorway, Jean Calmet had recognized the thick green book, on the only chair, at the side of the unmade bed.

"Who gave you that book?" Jean Calmet had asked, gasping. He had not even greeted Thérèse, had not taken her in his arms, nor placed a brief kiss on her sparkling temple.

"It's one of your students – Marc. I wanted to read *The Golden Ass*. Since the time that you spoke to me about it…"

"You could have asked me for it."

Jean Calmet was going to ask the question that was choking him:

"He brought it to you here?"

"He forgot to take it when he left. Does that bother you?"

The tramp. Well, that's that. It's all over. Now I don't have anything. Marc… Jean Calmet sees the handsome, insolent face, the forelock down over the nose, the eyes that burn with soft fire, the slow strides and the movements, so tender, so plain on the grave at Crécy… He feels the rending to the bottom of his soul.

"He spent the night here?"

"Goddamn it, Jean! I'm nineteen years old! I do what I please – understand? What I please!"

Her eyes full of lightning. The Cat Girl spits, she pulls back, she is going to spring. Marc on the gilded bedspread. Marc and the little coffee cups. Marc in the hollow of the bed. Marc crucified, Thérèse crawls over him, adorable succubus, ghoul on the move, vampire coiffed with light gold. Oh the little room is a castle on a forested mountain, an accursed fortress into which the bad genie draws the unfortunate passers-by! Witch, executioner, wicked fairy, the Cat Girl has the neighbourhood boys delivered, she grinds up their flesh, she feeds on it, she thrives on it, that blood-covered creature!

Thérèse does not fly at his face.

Jean Calmet walks to her.

Thérèse welcomes him, opens her arms, rubs her mouth against his throat, where his beard scratches a little, draws him onto the unmade bed. It is five o'clock, the end of the afternoon, the streets must be full of busy people. She puts Jean Calmet to bed like a baby, removes his clothing without haste, covers him with the sheet and the thick eiderdown, she undresses in her turn, lies down on him, encloses him like a sun shower. Marc's gaze is still fleeing. Fascinated, Jean Calmet could not take his eyes off the handsome, dark face, the restless forelock… Where was he last night? In the little room on the Rue de la Cité-Devant? It's a sure thing that they made love. All I have to do is turn my back and they get together. Marc, eighteen; Thérèse, nineteen…

The classroom was seething with excitement. The students interrupted one another. Tempers were rising. Their cheeks grew flushed with excitement. Jean Calmet was no longer trying to referee the debate. He was leaning at the back of the classroom, right next to Marc, with his elbow he was touching his thick woollen sweater and the boy did not move away, as if he were stupefied by fatigue. He woke up at the Café de l'Évêché, while the bells of the cathedral were striking noon, at Jean Calmet's table, when Thérèse, who had stopped on the threshold a moment, in the light, as if she were at the mouth of a shadowy grotto, spotted them and came towards them, laughing.

"Good morning, mister teacher, sir. Good morning, Marc."

She wore a white and yellow cashmere kerchief over her hair, like an icon. "Good morning, Marc..."

All three knew. Jean Calmet watched their eyes. Happy children. A boy from the Gymnase and a girl student at the École des Beaux-Arts. The three ate, Thérèse, Marc, Jean Calmet, then the children went back to school and Jean Calmet, who was off, returned to his residence, where he had letters to write and papers to mark.

He went out again about five o'clock and drank a beer. At the Brasserie de la Sallaz, before the window, a young man was making notes in a Bible. He was a bearded fellow, a shade over twenty, broad-shouldered, thoughtful, bespectacled, he read, he entered things in a notebook, he continued his reading, and, with a slim silver pencil, he made notes in the margin of the text and underlined long passages with the aid of a little ruler like those mathematicians and surveyors have. Jean Calmet looked at that bearded fellow with envy: despite the hubbub, the boy was absolutely isolated in his reading, absorbed in the text, possessed by the words like a hermit in his cell. He gave off an impression of compact strength and serenity. He went on writing in the margin of his Bible, underlining, writing briefly and carefully in his memo pad. Who was he? A theology student or perhaps some young probationary pastor in one of the parishes of La Sallaz or Chailly? It was Friday. No doubt he was preparing his Sunday sermon. Or was he one of those countless evangelists who scour the region, draw in young people and found disorganized communities which they hasten to leave for stable places? This fellow seemed too serious for the role. Perhaps a teacher then? Chaplain at an institution? At the House of Training in Vennes, for example? Jean Calmet shuddered. The House at Vennes had hung like a threat over his whole childhood. If you aren't nice, we'll put you in Vennes!... Oh, that kid, said the mother of one of the doctor's patients, a labourer at Paudex harbour who had trouble with his boy: he's at Vennes, of course! In those days, they used to speak of the "Reform School": Jean Calmet imagined the place full of naked children covered with welts, and brutes armed with birch rods and whips. As in an English print, which Jean Calmet had seen in one of the doctor's old books, the boys were tied to their beds, fastened to the wall with iron rings, beaten with riding crops, at the far end of the dormitory, by enormous, mirthful guards.

But there was nothing of the torturer about this bearded fellow. He read diligently with manifest serenity, and Jean Calmet wondered at the way that, thousands of years ago, the speeches of Moses, David or Solomon could captivate and fill a heart with fresh strength; that a parable of Jesus was capable of teaching the most everyday truth; that the accounts of the disciples or the letters of St Paul were as comforting as plain, solid dwellings, as actual facts. A breath passed over the tables of people drinking beer and white wine. A very ancient murmur haunted the café: God the poet, the God of words, was sending his Word through that little garnet Bible open beside a mug of beer, and millions of clamouring voices from the Old Testament repeated in their turn the Lord's word, the laments and praises of the Gospels sent back the echo of His voice.

Dumbstruck, Jean Calmet yielded to a catastrophic ecstasy, as if he had expected it for months. A brushwood bush blazed. Flowers filled up with blood. Armies of frogs invaded the streets and went into the houses. Clouds of mosquitoes came out of dust on the ground. Venomous flies emerged. The herds of May died at the side of the roads, the Jorat was nothing more than a stinking charnel house. Ulcers, pustules covered the limbs of all those that Jean Calmet had ever approached from far or near, as if they had to be punished for having met such a hopelessly guilty person. A huge cloud of hail suddenly burst over the region, massacring the already tall grass full of bellflowers and the orchards with shining petals. Then the whirling foehn threw tons of locusts on the towns and villages, they adhered to the ears and eyes of those who still dared to go outside. Jean Calmet's relatives, students – all the people he knew – were half-dead, on their knees, weeping and begging for mercy: a night thick as pea soup covered the land completely. It was sticky, it hung heavily, and when all the firstborn died at the same hour, Jean Calmet finally rejoiced at being the Benjamin of the tribe and at escaping for once the Lord's anger.

The fellow with the beard was still reading his Bible.

Jean Calmet had long since finished his beer. Where was Marc? Where was Thérèse? Were they making love under the gold-coloured bedspread? Naked, sweating, nimble, they traded their saliva, their young breath, and, from their bed, they heard the bells of the Gymnase every forty-five minutes. Jean Calmet bore them no grudge. He suffered. A needle pierced his heart when he imagined the embrace of shoulders and arms, Marc's black armpits glued to Thérèse's blonde armpits. A knifepoint drilled a hole in his skull when he remembered the smooth area, curved, evenly silvery around the childish little navel of Thérèse. The blade of an axe came down on his wrists, shearing his flesh to the bone the moment he remembered the very delicate toenails on the foot that Thérèse stretches towards him, from the far end of the bed: "Bite me," she said, "take my toes in your mouth, that's how it was when I was little, with my father, 'I want to eat you up,' he used to shout, it tickled, he would put my foot in his mouth, he used to bite, 'Ah, I'm hungry, I'm hungry,' he used to say, I really thought that he was going to swallow me whole!"

The picture brought back strange memories to Jean Calmet. It was a very old game, he must have been three or four years old, and he never remembered it without feeling again, shivering, the kind of horror with which the sound of the knife on the rough stone filled him. The doctor had just come home from his rounds, his face red, bathed in sweat, or his hair plastered down by the rain. They had finished supper, the older children had gone back up to their rooms, the maid was washing the dishes, Jean Calmet and his mother were the only ones left at the big table downstairs. The child was colouring pictures, humming, Madame Calmet was knitting. Suddenly, the car! The slamming door, the heavy, hurried footfalls on the gravel. The front door, noise in the vestibule, and the father comes into the room. His place is set at the head of the table, before the clock taller than him. He pats his wife's shoulder, he picks up Jean Calmet, turns him upside down, roughhouses with him, kisses him, corrects his drawing with one stroke, makes fun of him, kisses him again, puts down the child, who remains standing before the famished diner. Madame Calmet brings meat, pours another glass of wine.

"Why are you standing there before me?" exclaims the doctor, who stares into Jean Calmet's eyes while chewing his meat with gusto. A silence, during which the ferocious eyes do not leave him.

"I'm going to eat you up if you don't run away. I'm going to eat you for my supper, my little Jean!"

Jean Calmet cannot run away. Neither does he want to. He knows what comes next, he is waiting for it. He quivers with pleasure and fear thinking about it.

"So you don't want to hide! All right, you're going to see what you get!"

The doctor seizes the carving knife in his right hand and brandishes it before him; the blade sparkles. In his left hand he has his table knife, and slowly, carefully, he sharpens the two blades, rubbing them vigorously one against the other, while he makes cruel faces, rolls his eyes, shows his teeth, runs his tongue over his mouth.

"Ah! Ah!" he cries, making his voice deeper. "Ah, ah, ah, I'm going to eat you, Tom Thumb, I'm going to add you to my supper! See? I'm sharpening my big knife!"

And Jean Calmet looks with wonder at the blade shining and flashing under the lamp.

"Listen, the steel is growing sharper. Listen to that pretty concert!"

And Jean Calmet marvels at the hideous hissing of the two blades.

"Ah, ah, ah, the big man is going to eat the little boy who's dawdling in the forest!"

The doctor is still grinning. All of a sudden, with incredible agility, he throws out his paw, catches Jean Calmet by the nape of the neck, pulls the boy to him, bends him over his knees and places the cold blade on his throat.

"Well, now, my lamb!" cries the doctor. "We're going to cut his gullet! We're going to bleed this little fellow!"

The knifepoint pricks the skin, the doctor bears down a little, that is the game; the steel is driven a fraction of an inch into the skin, where a few little blood vessels yield almost at once. The doctor's left hand grips the frail shoulder. The right runs the knife over the white neck. The executioner growls and grumbles. The victim gives himself up and swoons with pleasure. At the far end of the room, in the dark, Madame Calmet, motionless, contemplates the ritual scene with an expressionless stare.

Now the doctor has released the child, he finishes his supper as if nothing had happened. There, it is all over. Besides, it is time to go to bed. Fearfully, Jean Calmet places a kiss on his father's cheek. And his mother takes him to his room upstairs, puts him to bed after a quick wash…

Jean Calmet paid for his beer and left. The street lights went on. Thérèse and Marc might have fallen asleep. Jean Calmet returned home and sat dreamily at his desk: by an ironic coincidence, on the pile of papers to be corrected, Marc's was the first. Jean Calmet read aloud: Marc Barraud, Latin translation, Classics 2G. M.T. Cicero: *De finibus*. He took the exercise, placed it before him, and, with a weary pen, he began to cross out in red the mistakes and mistranslations that the fatigue of love had prompted his blissful student to make.

The next day, which was a Saturday, an especially urgent and solemn teachers' conference took up the whole morning. Monsieur Grapp had convened it in response to the unrest that the recent events had spread among the teachers, staggered by the speed of the reactions of students and their overexcited parents. A painful session for Jean Calmet, who was struck dumb by a feeling of guilt at the back of the vast room, wainscoted and austere like a parish hall of the Église du Réveil. On their chairs – lined up as for a show – nearly a hundred fellow teachers were seated gravely. Even the youngest ones looked stern and tense. All of them were married or engaged; the few women in the gathering were unequivocally proper. Jean Calmet, for his part, was the rival of one of his students over a girl from the École des Beaux-Arts. Hubbub. Chairs pulled over the floor. At exactly fourteen minutes past eight, the Director made his entrance, and silence settled over the room. Monsieur Grapp took a seat at the big table that faced the rows of chairs, in the middle of the deans and the secretary, who was already busying himself with his papers.

Monsieur Grapp presided in a loud voice, and, on that morning, the memory of his still recent act charged his speech with convincing emotion. As he spoke, recounting the event in detail, analysing the circumstances, judging the reactions of the authorities and the public, he gained added sway over the assembly, where the sneers and sceptical looks of the leftists and the hotheads gave way to the worried faces of serious times. Member of the Vaud Council, staff colonel, Grapp was skilled at handling an assembly, and his stature – he was standing behind the table, dominating the room with his two hundred and twenty pounds – discouraged any uproar. Panic-stricken under an impressive face, Jean Calmet pondered the gulf that separated him from that man and from most of his fellow teachers. Here, everyone was in the service of order, which tolerated no deviation… And who am I? thought Jean Calmet. I'm adrift. I'm floundering. I'm going under. I'm hanging around. Exactly what my father used to say. I'm in love with a kid who's half my age. I'm fighting over her with a student. That's all it would take to ruin me for ever in the eyes of this assembly and the sacrosanct Board. And what a kid! Rather loud, and with the freedom of a tart. I'm in a mess again. What am I doing among these people? I'm fooling them all. I'll be punished. Besides, Grapp hasn't stopped looking at me. Why are people turning around to stare at me? They see my fears. I must be livid, yes, smeared with vile guilty fear. Guilty of what? After all, Thérèse is nineteen. So

I'm a bachelor? It isn't against the law. So I eat at the Café de l'Évêché with students? I don't do them any harm. On the contrary. But where does this fear of mine come from? I've been caught in the wrong. Found out. The principal's eyes on me. He has removed his dark glasses, he's holding them in his hand; I see his eyes that don't let me go. It's for me that he's speaking so loudly. It's me that he's warning, threatening! It's true – I must be filthy and slobbering with terror like a drunk who has just vomited and still has the puke on his lips, on his chin; when he opens his mouth you smell the sour odour of his debauchery, and it makes you want to vomit too. I stink with fear. That's my fate... And Jean Calmet, who does not recall that he is a good Latin master, that his students like him, that he serves the Gymnase perfectly, accuses himself and flogs himself at the back of the room, while his principal responds to the questions of the conference.

Sylvain Gautier, the fine Latinist, took the floor in his turn. A person with a white moustache, bent on convincing. There's a man who doesn't yield to anyone! Jean Calmet had him for a teacher at the secondary school, he knows his character – a solemn old Roman with a madness for integrity. When Sylvain sets eyes on him, Jean Calmet loses his composure and splutters just as in the small classroom, at the blackboard, during those terrible interrogations on Virgil or on Cicero. Then Verret, who does not talk much, let fly a few funny remarks. Little Beimberg, the aggressive mathematician with the curly brow of a ram, launched into a tribune's diatribe. Hulliger, the handsome Hellenist, summarized the situation very calmly. The ladies admired his silvery temples; and when Jaccoud asked for the floor in his turn, when he rose, glasses sparkling, chin thrust forward, canary-yellow vest, orange jacket, everyone imagined him, with his self-confidence and peremptory tone, in the role of the next principal. Jean Calmet admired and remained silent. They voted over and over again. Charles Avenex, a breezy hidalgo with the long neck of a sophisticated writer, rose to say that he understood nothing of what was transpiring. Jean Calmet smiled several times but he did not dare speak; his head aches, he is sweaty, he is bored to death; in the last row of the solemn room he ponders what it is that separates him from these people of faith.

The session lasted the whole morning. At noon, exhausted, Jean Calmet went home to bed, he slept and he had bad dreams. On waking he remembers one of them: he is naked, he is running in the courtyard of the Gymnase, the superintendent overtakes him and carries him gesticulating to the teachers' room, where, still naked and terrified with shame, he is forced to speak before their eyes, which will never forget his humiliation. Then Grapp shuts him up in his office, contemplates him affectionately and lends him an officer's overcoat to go home in.

Sunday, Montreux. Towards the mountains pigeons plunge into the green, towards the lake swans and gulls wage war on the water crested with gaseous foam by the north wind. An ominous arrival: beginning in Clarens, the mythological buildings, the towers, the battlements, the watchtowers, the balconies hung over the gardens of palm trees, Hôtel Rousseau, Hôtel Tilda, Lorius Hôtel; to the left, the Montreux Palace dotted with Swiss flags that are waving, behind them the snow of the mountains makes intense silvery stains, then there are more hotels, to the right the Casino and the skyscraper of the Eurotel, to the left the Hôtel de Londres, the Hôtel du Parc, to the right the Joli Site and the Métropole... The middle of town.

Jean Calmet parks his car at the covered market: a kiosk of metal, pipe scaffolding, bolts like hilarious faces, slopes of aluminium and cast iron, which recall an operetta railway station and a humbled pagoda. Jean Calmet walks along the embankment: low palm trees with fronds erect as brooms, magnolias in blossom, star-shaped daffodils, mimosas that move about like chicks at the end of their slender branches, pink gravel, tulips of a coaly mauve, and suddenly, leaning against a Bernese chalet with rustic, overhanging eaves, a mosque covered with blue and white tiles that brings into this bay of Nice a bedlam of panic-stricken camels, curved-knife vengeance and holy war against a background of the sandy, illiterate Middle Ages. The edifice displays its name over the door: Le Hoggar. Jean Calmet enters, climbs a few steps, makes his way into a cathedral of decorated nougat, with a ceiling like an immense ray of white honey, from which hang wire-bound brass lamps. The floor is a kaleidoscope nocturnal and cool with stars, moons; tender, welling drops of water on the deep green, like eyes that do not let it fall. Pieces of Turkish delight are lying on trays. In niches gleam water jugs painted yellow and blue. Round chapels open out at the back, behind portcullises. Reedy music sustained by tambourines fills the establishment with an unbroken monotony. Without malice, from a heavily veiled girl whose fingernails, painted a purple that is almost black, make him think of the tulips along the embankment, Jean Calmet orders the worst thing in the world: a barely potable mint tea that he forces himself to ingurgitate with a gloomy, sickeningly sweet hunk of Turkish delight.

When he goes out again, on the canal which runs along the western flank of the mosque, he sees a black woman with a red turban walking on the arm of a boxing champ from Montreux whom he knows by sight. Jean Calmet thinks that, in the grey of the canal protected from the light of the lake, the black woman is bearing the disc of the setting sun balanced on her head.

Towards Savoy, the sky is silky, dazzling.

Gulls soar, lines of molten metal. A flock of pigeons with flapping wings circles between the ugly old buildings with

Neapolitan tiles over the sewery water of the canal. Few passers-by. The woman and the boxer are sitting on a bench near the clumps of palm trees. The lake is turning green. The glacial north wind whips up the waves like small Alps among the red and blue hulls of boats, all of whose registration numbers begin with the victorious V of the canton of Vaud. In the distance the tiny steamer slides before the French coast. On the rooftops of hotels, the wind bites into the banners of Swiss crimson with the white cross. Coots scream, plunge, scream again. Jean Calmet is not impatient. He has a date with Thérèse at six o'clock.

He finds her at the Café Apollo. When he enters, she is already seated close to the front window; he notices that she is outlined against the lake and the pink sky just at the level of the roof of the covered market where pigeons pursue one another. The little round wicker basket lies next to her on the bench; she has her iconic kerchief; she is reading a paperback.

Jean Calmet draws near, she raises calm, green eyes to him, he brushes her lips with a kiss, he sits down beside her, he places his hand on the round basket.

"Your mother all right?"

"You know," she said, "I didn't see much of her, it's always the same, she complains about not seeing me all week, and as soon as I'm here, she disappears, she sees friends, it seems like she takes advantage of the weekend to run every which way…"

"And what did you do, Thérèse?"

"I slept, I read, I ate, I went for a walk around Montreux. I always feel funny being in Montreux. I feel like a child again. I went walking in the yard of the Collège. It's stupid, right? I guess I'm really sentimental… And then I made a drawing. Here, I brought it for you."

She unfolds a white paper that she has slipped among the pages of her book, she sets it before Jean Calmet. It is a cat drawn with a green ballpoint pen – two immense, staring cat's-eyes that transpierce Jean Calmet with their white fire. For a moment he sees only those dilated pupils, those irises that search him. Cat-Inquisitor. Cat-Judge. He hates it instantly. Then he sees the cat's feathery cheeks, its pointed ears, its forked moustache: the green ink has striped, pricked, scratched the picture with slight wounds that spread in a star towards the edges of the paper like explosions or rays, which the eye follows almost painfully. Wicked cat. Something is written in tiny letters under the vile beast. Jean Calmet has trouble making it out, for the fur and its crackling halo mingle with the text. He manages to read: *One night in Montreux – done in the morning before the open window,* and he wonders immediately what those innocent words conceal. At any rate, the cat is detestable: without saying anything, Jean Calmet folds it into quarters and slips it into his wallet.

"Excuse me a moment," says Thérèse, who gets to her feet and heads for the toilets.

Jean Calmet is alone, he places his hand on the little round basket. With his palm, he tests the gentleness of the wicker flanks, the roundness of the lid secured to the basket by a loop. With his fingers, he follows the stalks of wicker, goes down into the hollows, comes back up, runs under another strand, returns to the first; he thinks about Little Red Riding Hood in the woods, about the basket hung over the little girl's arm; it is a tender, heart-rending picture, the gift, a dream sprung from the bottom of childhood under the pine trees, where the night thickens, the little boots creep along the path, one hears the more and more hurried breath of the girl who rushes into the twilight... How many fresh little baskets are crossing how many forests at just this moment. How many wolves lying in wait. The child starts to run, she pants. The cottage is still so far away! Jean Calmet sees the child's clear eyes, the blue gaze, the black gaze that becomes anxious, the little nose that wrinkles up, the mouth lacking a tooth, which has just fallen out, the angel's mouth in which a sob is rising...

Thérèse still does not come back. Jean Calmet takes the little basket on his lap, he opens it, he glances into its disorder. Right on top is a wrinkled handkerchief marked "M.B." This handkerchief wounds Jean Calmet. He takes hold of it: the handkerchief is compact, as if starched. He lifts it to his nose: the handkerchief smells of dry sperm. That odour of rancid milk, dried fish, feverish night... A handkerchief full of sperm. Marc's sperm. His student in Classics 2G. Marc Barraud, eighteen years old, Avenue de Beaumont, 57, Lausanne. Jean Calmet puts back the stiff handkerchief, he closes the lid, he sets the basket on the bench beside him.

Thérèse comes out of the toilets, she smiles at him from afar; he sees her litheness, her loose-limbed movements, her long hair that streams down over her delicate shoulders. She sits down.

"What if we take a walk?" she asks.

Now Jean Calmet's voice is hoarse.

"Seen Marc this weekend?"

"He came by to say hello yesterday. Saturday is fun. There's dances, merry-go-rounds..."

She has not lied. She speaks with a naturalness that pierces Jean Calmet's heart. He has lost her. He knows it. He knows that he will remember hideously that moment when the ground gives way. He will remember, as he falls, that through the café window he notices:

an ice-cream vendor with a little white cart
a Mercedes with German plates that is moving at six
    miles an hour looking for a parking space
a meter inspector with a pencil behind his ear

a boxer dog pissing against a hydrant
the palm trees on the embankment
the greyish roof of the covered market
the disc of the sun perfectly red in the orange sky.

Thérèse falls silent. Jean Calmet does not speak any more. He pays, he gets to his feet, he holds open the door, he follows Thérèse onto the square. The car is a two-seater. During the ride, Thérèse hugs the little basket to her like a baby that she is protecting. A half-hour's ride and Jean Calmet drops her off at La Cité. Her eyes are full of tears.

"Want to come up for a minute?"

He melts. He is saved. He locks the car, he follows Thérèse up the narrow staircase. Her door. Her key. They enter. In the room she sets the basket down on the floor; quickly she lights a candle, and the bedspread radiates with all its gold in the semidarkness.

They stretch out one against the other, and on the moss of her temples, in the labyrinth of her ears, on the smooth areas of her neck, Jean Calmet breathes the perfume of cinnamon, of very faint perspiration, of a flowering swamp in the noonday light: in her hair he finds the odour of the amber-coloured flint that they look for in the quarries, that they strike against a twin rock; a small column of smoke rises from the shock, and the stone that they lift to their nostrils begins smelling of tepid fire like a memory of the planet's first cataclysms.

The pink obscurity closed in, a draught made the candle flame tremble.

Sweetness. Jean Calmet crucified flat on the bed, once again, Thérèse lies down on him, draws him into her, for a long, long time devours him with tenderness, then she raises herself, slides out of the embrace, she straightens up, she is kneeling, her thighs parted, she leans out of the bed, even if he closes his eyes he knows that she is reaching out gropingly, she finds the little basket, she opens it, she takes Marc's handkerchief, she leans back a little and wipes herself quickly – the handkerchief makes a brittle sound in the wet night.

Marc. Jean Calmet will have him for the first hour tomorrow, they will read the rest of the *Metamorphoses* of Apuleius. Thinking about Marc does not hurt, just now. And Thérèse, the Cat Girl, the witch, the succubus, the terrible silky fairy lies down beside him again, she places the handkerchief under the pillow; with his finger Jean Calmet tests it – rigid, gluey, flattened under the head with the radiant hair. The candle is still burning. Jean Calmet draws her to him, blows out the flame; given off at once is the odour of the hot wax and of the wick that is charring: the smell of Christmas! says Thérèse. They fall asleep. Tonight Jean will have no nightmares.

Some time had gone by since Jean Calmet had seen his mother, and it made him suffer like he had committed an act of cowardice. As he was off the following Thursday, he went down to Les Peupliers to pay her a visit. They talked for an hour; Madame Calmet wanted to know how Jean was living, where he took his meals, if he gave out his laundry to be done. She told him about his brothers and sisters, she babbled a little, she looked like a grey mouse, her small round eyes without expression. While she was making tea in the kitchen, Jean Calmet came across an open newspaper in the middle of sewing boxes, on the veranda: *The Cremation*, "organ of the Cremation Society of the Canton of Vaud, published four times yearly."

"What's this rag?" he asked his mother, intrigued.

"I've been getting it since Papa died. I joined the Society, you know. You pay only twenty francs a year and they handle all the formalities, the crematorium, settling all the bills. Can you imagine that? Instead of having to pay eight hundred or a thousand francs, like everyone else, you pay only twenty francs a year, it's quite a saving. Pity we didn't know about it for Papa's death. It was after the ceremony that they came to talk to me about it..."

Jean Calmet felt acute discomfort. He opened the newspaper, instantly spotted the Society's device – the same as the one which decorated the pediment of the crematorium with its big Roman letters:

PER IGNEM AD PACEM

and a sinister vignette showed flames spurting from a kind of alcohol-fried chafing dish against a black background.

"You read this in detail?" he asked.

"From cover to cover," replied his mother. "It's very interesting and thorough."

Jean Calmet shivered. He began to perspire on the veranda overheated by the afternoon sun; the heavily sweetened tea nauseated him. He skimmed through the newspaper, he read:

In case of death outside the Canton of Vaud, in Switzerland or abroad, our society gives the family a reimbursement equal to the amount that it would have spent if the incineration had taken place in the Canton, i.e. cost of incineration, cost of coffin, shipping charges from the border of Vaud to the nearest crematorium, organist's services.

With regard to the shipping of ashes, it is possible to send these to Switzerland, by mail, without difficulty...

and he imagined the postman's face when, on the arrival of the bound parcel, a thin trickle of velvety ash begins to run, and he instantly gathers it up and brings it to the deceased's family. He had to make an effort to remind himself that his father's ashes were shut up in an urn behind the padlocked grating of a columbarium guaranteed by the police administration. He went back to the newspaper. On the first page, a member had sent in a little poem, 'The Last Fire', which ended with these lines:

> *If by fire we are consumed,*
> *Then ashes suddenly are we!*
> *But in earth where we lie buried,*
> *What shall we be next summer?*
> *Let us not impose gardening*
> *On those who have seen us die!*

Jean Calmet dropped the horrible sheet, but his mother picked it up, folded it respectfully and set it clearly in sight on the table. In spite of himself, from his seat, he read another fragment of an article that was bathed in the yellow four-o'clock sun:

First, we'll talk about France. In Paris, the hall of ceremonies comprises two hundred seats (chairs and armchairs). It is sumptuously decorated with mosaics and a sculptural composition: 'The Return of the Eternal'. One of the clauses of the decree of 31 December 1941 expressly states: "Immediately after incineration, the ashes are to be gathered in an urn in the presence of the family." The persons attending the services do not leave the crematorium before the restitution of the ashes. This waiting period varies from fifty to sixty minutes.

He paused, took a sip of tea, resumed reading the paper:

Strasbourg – There are two chapels: one with three hundred seats and the other with eighty. The main hall has an organ, the small one a harmonium. The ceremonies are identical, regardless of which hall is used.

The day before or two days before the service, the coffin is generally placed in the refrigerated cellars of the crematorium. An hour before the beginning of the ceremony, the coffin is set on a catafalque, the latter being covered by a pall embroidered with gold. A podium is available to any speakers for religious or secular speeches. A charge is made for the use of the organ or harmonium. Strasbourg has no columbarium.

He became excited, he turned the page. The doctor's silhouette appeared, massive, before the big clock.

Marseille – The coffin, covered with a black pall with gold fringe, is placed on a catafalque in the centre of a large hall furnished with benches. Two hundred persons can be seated there. A well-placed rostrum allows any speakers to make themselves heard easily. No music is possible. The coffin is brought by pall-bearers into the adjacent room, where the ovens are located.

The persons attending the services may then leave, but they may also wait (about an hour) for the return of the urn, either remaining inside the crematorium or going out into the neighbouring cemetery. Covered with the pall, the urn is borne on a small litter, then placed in the columbarium or transported to another place…

That was too much. Furious, Jean Calmet crumpled the crackling double sheet, made it into a ball and hurled it into a corner of the veranda, behind a colony of green plants.

"What's wrong with you?" Madame Calmet said timidly. "Did something offend you?"

What was the good of replying? He was humiliated by his act. He looked at the bent old woman in anger; it grieved him that she was his mother, that she must die, that she too would be reduced to ashes before he could tell her at least a part of what had been oppressing him for years. Did she suspect anything? Had she guessed, deep in her heart, the anguish of her Benjamin, his terrors, his need for affection, that hunger torturing him body and soul? Then Jean Calmet did something that he had never done, that he had never even dreamt of doing: he rose, he walked towards his mother, he lifted her from her armchair, and he embraced her, pressed her against him, slight, bony, he hugged the ridiculous little being who did not struggle, who did not react; she simply allowed herself to be squeezed to the point of breathlessness, she puffed harder, Jean Calmet thought of Thérèse's panting under the golden bedspread. You, too, have been Ophelia, he pondered, hugging the emaciated body; you, too, have enchanted, soothed, cherished, you were Circe, Melusina, you were Morgana, you were all the fairies in the tales, and now your bones jut out and the wrinkles lacerate your face!

Suddenly Jean Calmet remembered a boarding house in Corbeyrier, where he had spent a few weeks in the winter with his mother when he was small. They would gather in a tidy, low parlour, on straw chairs; groups of ladies and bronchitic kids played cards, the golden crusts of the leftovers from supper and café au lait still lay about under the chandeliers of the glass-enclosed dining room. Papa would send postcards from Lutry. On the morning of 1 January, the owner had executed a wildcat with buckshot in the snow-covered hedge. He had aimed at it for a long time. Jean Calmet was seven years old, he could not turn the rifle aside; the animal, wounded in the throat, fell on the ground, plop, they had picked it up from the frozen gravel that stuck to the earth and they had thrown it into an open garbage can in front of the pension. Jean Calmet used to cough at night. His mother would get out of bed; the chafing dish was out, she would give him what was left of the cold cough mixture. He used to dream of a poster for Player's cigarettes that showed a blond, pasty-faced doll-woman in the snow; such faces are seen, even nowadays, on the mannequins of cheap clothing stores. In the afternoon, after the midday nap, a little girl – also seven – would pee in a chamber pot without closing her door. Jean Calmet waited for the ceremony of the toilet paper, the cotton underpants and the gaiters...

"You're angry about the newspaper?" asked a frail voice. Jean Calmet had felt the weak torso vibrate with the tremor of the voice.

No, he wasn't angry. He was shocked, uneasy. He was no longer thinking about it. His mother's small body, her protruding shoulder blades, the rabbit's ribs had filled him with another anguish. He bent down, he brushed his lips over the forehead criss-crossed with tiny star-shaped wrinkles. Towards her temples, a lock of white hair stuck out and tickled his lips unpleasantly.

"You know, since Papa was burned, I get a pile of things that I knew nothing about. And I've joined the Society, thinking that I'll be needing it before long."

A silence. The pair were still standing in the light that was turning brown.

"Staying for supper?"

The voice trembled. It was a humble query, an entreaty, she did not dare believe that he would: Jean is wild, Jean always runs away; even when he was a child she used to call him the little Cat that Walked by Himself... Poor old voice. Poor bent skeleton, poor imploring face, poor gaze dimmed with tears, vacant, grey, bluish, washed out by the years of obedience. She would die. You, too, my beloved, at the crematorium...

God is a bastard.

Jean Calmet left Les Peupliers before supper. He would not have had the strength to eat sitting across from this old woman with her slow movements: this hand that can no longer cut the meat, this mouth that drools a little, that hisses when chewing, this noisy mouth...

While he was going back up to town, he was followed by the worn-out gaze as by a very old reproach: the iris that had been forget-me-not blue and that had faded, that had grown pale, that had begun to resemble the gaze of the blind – but perhaps it is because the heart now sees into it clearer and deeper than any eye? Jean Calmet mused and saw again scenes of his childhood. Then he recalled the knots of arthritis on the old hands, brownish speckles, nearly violet stains. Soon she will lose her memory, she will confuse everything, she will no longer be able to find her way about alone... Her master is dead. She must die. Who will close the eyes of the poor shrivelled-up thing on her pillows? Jean Calmet choked at the wheel of the Simca, which moved ahead ten yards at a time in the crowded streets of the evening.

During this time, the Gymnase had set up a day for study trips all over the country, and 2G, Jean Calmet's class, wanted to go to Bern, a bit derisively, a bit out of an old, atavistic respect, but also an ironic way to make fun of the Swiss capital, its banks, its big hotels, its stodginess, its dialects that resemble Dutch.

"Can we take along friends?"

Jean Calmet had agreed.

They were to meet in the main terminal of the Gare de Lausanne. One fine morning at the end of May, they assemble wearing cowboy hats, Indian neckerchiefs, boots; they carry US Army knapsacks full of comic books and cartons of cigarettes. A few guests in the bunch: boys from the École des Beaux-Arts, two girls from the École Normale... A few yards away, François Clerc assembled his students.

"Where are you going?" asks Jean Calmet.

"To Payerne. The Abbey Church, you know, the museum, then a walk over the hills..."

François smiles when Jean Calmet tells him that he is going to Bern.

"You're going to steep yourself in the Federal mystique?"

To be sure, this Bernese project makes everyone laugh. Jean Calmet is somewhat stung, even if he is having fun, even if he is laughing, too. He knows all too well that Bern vaguely intimidates him: the authority of Bern, its history as father and cement of the Confederation, its military power, its alliances, the execution of its enemies in the subjugated territories, the mystery, too, of those phrases so often repeated on the shores of Lake Léman and in such a tone of respect and childish irritation: "*They* decided, in Bern... Go ask Bern for it... The Federal Council has voted... Bern demands..."

He came back to his students, counted them with a discreet glance. Marc was missing. Would he come? Jean Calmet was getting ready to go to Platform I when, at the last minute, a very handsome couple came through the great glazed portal: Marc and Thérèse. Jean Calmet gulped, a lump came into his throat; he began to tremble, but his eyes did not leave the couple that came dancing across the waiting room, which was full of noise.

They were holding hands.

They had no bags.

Marc, thin and long, the lock of hair on his cheek, his face and hands tanned, his body lithe, and his legs slim in the patched trousers!

Thérèse had untied her braid. The copper flood fell in two cascades on her bare shoulders. She was wearing a little white blouse with gold thread; her thighs, her legs stretched the cloth of the jeans at every step.

They come up to Jean Calmet smiling with graciousness. They shake hands with him, talk to him!

Jean Calmet mumbles words of greeting, nervously counts his tickets again, it seems to him that he is unsteady, that he may faint on the spot: "Let's go," he says in the black light.

Platform brutally light, big green train, stamping of feet along the walkway, reserved coach, bounding onto the platform, races, cries, calls. Jean Calmet was pinned between Béatrice and Daisy; across from him Christophe unwrapped packs of chewing gum and offered them all around. Jean Calmet has closed his eyes, he plunges into opaque birdlime, he chokes. Marc and Thérèse. The whole day. They get out of bed. They come gambolling down from the Place de la Cité to the station. Hand in hand. Radiant in the early morning, in the wind from the lake still cool from the mountain night of Savoy and from the flatlands on the banks of the Rhône. And he, Jean Calmet, lonely and glum before them! He felt spite and anger. Towards them, towards himself, towards the light and towards the wind that was flying through the compartment, all the windows of which were open. For a moment, he was away in the acrid mud. He splashed and floundered. He sank into it. He died of shame...

When he reopened his eyes, the train was crossing the green plateau before the Bernese Alps, which were all white like the ones on wrappers of chocolate: meadows, villages, blue woods, more pastures, huge, flowered, overgrown, and the emerald shadow at the edges of the fields. Marc and Thérèse were standing at a window, their hair mingling; Marc had put his arm over her bare shoulders. He squeezed that sweetness against him, he screwed up his eyes against the wind, he would often place his head on the neck of Thérèse and caress his forehead, his nose, his lips against her skin streaming with the morning air.

"Deer! Deer!"

Three animals had bounded out of a wood; they skirted the edge of the fields with great leaps, disappeared in the brush.

Marc and Thérèse raised the window and sat, one against the other, their legs stretched out, feet up on the seat across the way. How good-looking they are, thought Jean Calmet. How innocent they are. Marc is the lover of Thérèse. When I tried to love her, I was impotent and ridiculous. Im-po-tent. I'm miserable. I'm jealous. My God, what have I done that you take everything from me? I'm wrapped up in myself, separated from the others, deprived, guilty, because of Your Law, which I submit to like a humiliated child. Will the barrier fall? Will sweetness be given to me, rendered up to me, before the final plunge into darkness?

They reached Bern.

At once, the city seemed solemn and in good health. A weight fell on their shoulders: eight centuries of power and indestructible vigour. They did not sing any more. It took a few moments to recover from the shock. They reached the heart of town: Marktgasse, Bärenplatz; all of a sudden the cupolas of the Federal Palace shone in the blue sky. Columns, monumental staircases, high walls, outbuildings, verdigris roofs; with absolute certainty the edifice expressed strength, perpetuity, faith in democratic virtue, domestic wisdom, contempt for fashions. All of it squat, close-set, and breathing at the same time, flanked by huge, solemn banks, the health of an old man vigorous and thriving on his heap of gold.

That power irritated Jean Calmet. Now his students had begun to laugh again. They deciphered, amid gibes, the patriotic devices and the cantonal coats of arms of the ornamental pediments. Some of them intoned revolutionary songs, into which they mockingly slipped fragments of hymns of sacred Switzerland; others essayed a dance step, miming drunkards stunned by so much splendour. The mirth was at its height when a detachment of cadets, led by a little captain of dragoons, came out on the square at a ceremonial step. "*Zu miiin' Befehl, halt!*" Forty stiff caps, visors pulled down over their domes, forty uniforms gleaming like pistachio candy, then the "Attention!" that cracks and echoes several times among the colonnades of the holy square. Thirty yards away, Jean Calmet and his class heard the guttural dialect of the officer, who became ecstatic and revealed the endless mysteries of the Palace.

They walked, they went down little arcaded streets, they took a break under a clock from which emerged and strutted characters in costumes of pomp and coupled wagons. They went past still other banks, which mystically reproduced the pediment-cupola-column style of the Federal temple; they stopped in front of embassies, whose iron gates, coats of arms and armoured limousines with whitewall tyres in the courtyard of honour had them dreaming up parodies of espionage films. They bought beer and frankfurters at refreshment stands, they ate and drank in the open air, congregating on the green benches of a mall overlooking the Aar, they threw their empty bottles into the river, they got themselves bawled out by the park attendant who called them "*Frenchy* students," they sang a stanza of 'L'Internationale' at the top of their lungs right in the face of the very sheepish, shocked old man; finally they arrived at the Bear Pit, and they were happy at once, they enjoyed themselves with genuine pleasure that seemed to come from their very recent childhoods. It was a broad stone-walled pit, divided into several airy territories, at the centre of which a big, dry tree that was scratched all over stood like a tortured prisoner. At the bottom of the pit, in the first cavity, a very tall, very dark, plump bear, his shoulders humped with fat, stood and implored the spectators, making a comic imitation of a man who is praying, who clasps his hands, who spreads them apart, who again makes a gesture of supplication. He rolled his round eyes, but his defiant, cruel bearing, his sharp teeth, the thread of drool on his long, mobile snout, his claws above all, long and curved like blades of black steel, gave him a look of paradoxical, comic ferocity. He danced, he grunted, he waddled about on his formidable hind legs. A fellow tossed him a handful of carrots; the bear dropped back down with suppleness, they heard his claws lacerate the ground, he ran to the feast, he gobbled up the carrots noisily. Jean Calmet remembered what they had told him, as a child, one day when he had come to see the Pit with his parents: a kid had fallen into it, the keeper had gone away to do some shopping, nobody had been able to act, the child had been devoured by the huge bear under the horrified gaze of his parents and the crowd! The doctor had not spared him a single detail, boasting of the bear's speed, its extraordinary voracity. "And you know," he had added, staring curiously at his own son, "he devoured the boy whole; at the end of the meal there was nothing left but his two shoes." The doctor once more. His father once more. Could it be he, that muscular, insatiable male at the bottom of the pit? Had he reappeared once more, to oppress his youngest child? Nothing but his two shoes! Terror-stricken, Jean Calmet relived the paternal narrative, re-experiencing his terror of that day, despite himself seeking on the cobblestones – covered with fresh excrement and the remains of vegetables – traces of the horrible meal, bloodstains, and the two innocent little shoes that the animal had not wanted.

But his students gave admiring shouts from the other side of the ramp. The girls called to him; he went around the pits and joined them before an odd and cunning spectacle that made him forget the image of the bloody scene. A big she-bear good-naturedly nudged three cubs with her snout. The white-collared cubs trotted, rolled over, jumped on one another, tripped one another, abruptly ran away, galloped, came back under the paws and snout of their mother with obvious pleasure. The she-bear swung her head right and left, watching over her offspring, apparently laughing. Yes, everyone could see it: she was laughing, her muzzle opened for a blissful enchantment that delighted the onlookers. A swipe of her paw sent one of the young flying like a ball against the sandstone: astonished, perhaps in pain, the cub gave a raucous bellow and sat, dazed, in the sun, when its mother called to it with a kind of plaintive bleat.

Jean Calmet stopped looking at the animals to turn towards his students. Leaning over the edge, glued to the stone, their nails instinctively digging into it, they followed the animals' movements with extraordinary curiosity. Suddenly Jean Calmet felt himself grow pale; he was cold, nausea hurled a handful of acid into his stomach: on the other side of the Pit, outlined against the sky, intertwined, marvellous, Marc and Thérèse had appeared. They stood there, hugging each other; their hair streamed in the breeze, their well-attuned bodies looked alike, their heads leant one towards the other before the sparkling sky... Jean Calmet was unsteady. He closed his eyes. He opened them again. The couple was still there, as if to remind him of his failure the first time that he had slept with Thérèse. As if to remind him of his age. To keep him away from the little room in La Cité. To forbid him to see the girl again...

Despondent, he felt in his heart and his mind all the knives of jealousy. It made him ashamed, because he was really in love and because he had tender feelings towards Thérèse and Marc. Yes, he was ashamed, that shame grieved him, but a confused clamour within him cried things that grew distinct, that became hard, that solidified disgustingly: "Impotent! Useless! Jealous! What are you waiting for to get out of the way once and for all?" He staggered under the insults. "To get out of the way! Do you hear, imbecile? You should have got it through your head long ago!"

150

They gathered, they started to walk again through the little streets. The afternoon was turning a sepia gold: in the sky a tint of brown sugar, heavy, a bit soporific. They were about to reach a bridge guarded by obelisks when the class stopped and stared at a stupefying monument. Shouts and laughter mingled. Jean Calmet, who had been walking like a somnambulist for a moment, lifted his eyes and was struck with amazement: an Ogre was sitting at the top of the shaft of a fountain, devouring an already half-swallowed child whose bare buttocks and little dimpled thighs thrashed about on his bloody chest! Jean Calmet screwed up his eyes to see better: the scene was dreadful. Thick-set, his face broad, his mouth distended, immense, his wide-spaced teeth planted in the child's back, the Ogre showed mute pleasure, and his flat nose, his blue eyes, the whole rictus of his face insulted the passers-by compelled to witness his crime. One realized, to see him so sure of himself, greedy and vigorous, that nothing could stop his odious banquet. The monster was comfortably seated, wearing a blood-red tunic and green breeches spotted with horrible, rust-like spatterings. His right elbow raised on high, with his huge paw he held the naked kid in his gaping, crimson mug. Under his left arm, a supply of fresh flesh: a plump little girl with long hair, her face distorted by screams and tears; poor little victim, all ready to be gobbled up at the next meal. In the Ogre's belt, still on the left, a sack from which emerged the torsos of crying boys and girls. They were very pale, and their skin made a strange contrast with the killer's coppery hide. The little boy had managed to get out of the basket as far as his belly, he was trying to escape, he made a terrific effort, he clung to the Ogre's leg to help himself, and this useless attempt, the tears, the little body that was writhing added to the horror of the giant, whose feast nothing could stop. Another kid was hung from his belt, to the right, next to the butcher's knife. This child also struggled, lashing out with his little legs against the knee of the monstrous character, who must have liked this gesticulation, who enjoyed it, who was impatient to taste that nice living flesh which was twisting in its bonds and in its baskets: that is why he always had his larder with him, securely lashed to his belt; the fresh meat lived and moved on his own hip, against his own skin, whetting his appetite, provoking his laughter. The Ogre's mirth! For Jean Calmet had just made an appalling discovery: the Ogre looked like his father. Could the Ogre be his father, a new image of his father risen up from the crematorium to warn him again and persecute him? It was the doctor all right, those broad shoulders, that strong back, that jovial, cruel thickness of his whole body. It was him all right – that confidence in the face of disaster, that insolent voracity, those blue eyes defying the world like all-powerful fires, that laugh on his face and on his wide-spaced teeth under his big lips. Jean Calmet remembered the evening ritual, the hissing of the sharpened knives one against the other:

"That child is so cute I'd eat him. I'm going to gobble him up raw!"

And the grunts, the drools, the mimicry of impatience and appetite accompanied ferociously the sharpening, and the doctor's big hand squeezed Jean Calmet's throat, immobilizing him on knees as hard as those of the dirty statue...

Jean Calmet realized that he had forgotten his students. They were having fun splashing one another with the water from the fountain; others, at the stand across the way, were buying postcards of the scene: *Kindlifresserbrunnen* they spelled out diligently. The Fountain of the Devourer of Small Children! The Fountain of the Cannibal! And Jean Calmet remembered Chronos, who had devoured his offspring alive, the fantastic Saturn swallowing his offspring alive, Moloch thirsty for the blood of innocent young men, the terrible tax of fresh meat that Crete paid to the divine Minotaur at the bottom of his labyrinth streaming with haemoglobin. Jean Calmet's father had devoured him, too. Wolfed him down. Reduced him to nothing. He was filled with violent hatred for the Ogre-doctor, for all the other ogres who had massacred their sons, their children, the tributes constantly renewed with young flesh, minced meat, flesh of pleasure, cannon fodder, all that flesh that they had appallingly sacrificed generation after generation to live on, to enjoy, to thrive on, to aggrandize themselves! Gilles de Rais! Elizabeth Báthory, marten thirsty for wailing! And you, huntsmen of Leipzig and of Mayence, lying in ambush in your haunts and staring at the night with a pink eye; you, the cutters of girls, the prowlers of operating rooms, the robbers of children, whom you shove into your game bags in the dusk of the evening! You, marrow-swallowers, blood-suckers, all the vampires, all the butchers, dismemberers, sawyers, cutters of chubby big-bottomed kids, lickers of bloody dimples, slaughterers of angels, disembowellers of virgins sticky with vermilion! Staring at the statue of the killer, Jean Calmet saw stretching out a whole gallery venomous and foaming with red. And his father was the last monster of that abominable line! And Jean Calmet had had to be handed over as youngest son, bound hand and foot, completely at the Ogre's mercy, weak, motionless, impotent!

Impotent.

That was it all right. By terrifying him, devouring him, seizing him like an object that he ground up, that he bled as he pleased, the doctor had tried to sterilize him to keep his potency as father, as hard authoritarian chief, which he had to retain at any cost. His brothers had fled. His sisters had fled. He had remained in the Master's power, he, Jean Calmet, and he had been murdered.

Now the young people were growing impatient; evening was falling on the city. They headed back to the station. Turning around, Jean Calmet threw a last look at the Ogre, who went on imperturbably with his ignoble feast.

His heart was full of bitterness and rage. What an indignity. Thérèse and Marc were walking ahead of him. They had their arms around each other's waists. Jean Calmet watched their slim buttocks move in their identical jeans, their slender, muscular legs, their tread. For a moment, he imagined the two young people handed over to the priests of Moloch or Baal. He saw Thérèse, half-naked, gesticulate in the Ogre's wicker pack. He heard Marc's cries as the giant squeezed his throat, crushed it, as Saturn does in his cavernous maw! The boy's legs moved grotesquely in mid-air; streams of his precious blood ran over the tunic of the famished executioner! And if he doesn't die as an executed prisoner, he will wind up as dust, like the others, or in a hole, rotten; his limbs will come off and sink in the wet earth. Poor Marc. It's just a question of years. Baal or the scythe…

With these sad thoughts, Jean Calmet recognized his jealousy, and he was humiliated by their baseness. Thérèse had not said a word to him all day. Nor given him a single look. He came back to his loneliness as to an inborn defect. Who would ever give him back his life? He became an ogre in his turn. He began to muse over sacrifices, he heard the cracking of the bones of the ones who had rejected him, he buried them nastily… He was afraid, he was cold. They reached the station. The street lights went on. The beautiful children sang as they boarded the train.

Part IV
The Immolation

I have said to corruption: Thou art my father…

Job 17:14

ONE EVENING, SOME TIME LATER, Jean Calmet was drinking a beer alone at the Lyrique when the café door opened on a person he avoided seeing, and whom he pretended not to recognize, afterwards, when the other, from his seat, would not stop looking at him, trying to attract his attention. The fellow had ordered a beer, too; he drank with a hurried look, paid, slipped back into his raincoat: just as he was leaving, he made a sudden turn and came up to Jean Calmet, his hand outstretched.

"You remember me, don't you?"

Jean Calmet remembered him all too well.

It was that skinny fellow, George Mollendruz.

Mollendruz, the leader of a tiny Hitlerian group that had had trouble with the police.

Mollendruz, who put out – at his own expense – a little neo-Nazi newspaper, *The True Europe*, in which a few persons, nostalgic for the pomp of pre-war Nuremberg and for the final solution, belched forth.

Annoyed, Jean Calmet stretched out a reticent hand to him. The other took it – his palm was moist – and sat down without waiting for an invitation.

"You'll have a beer, won't you, Monsieur Calmet? This round is on me!"

His voice attempted cordiality, but, for a few moments, Jean Calmet felt an anguish that continued to grow: Mollendruz's faded eyes were staring at him with disagreeable curiosity, his hands trembled continually... Mollendruz made sad company: people took him for a miserable, feeble-minded character. Jean Calmet had known him in the bistros when he was a student. They were about the same age. In those days, Mollendruz campaigned in a Lake Léman section of the Arrow Cross Party, and he had displayed photos of Hitler before the eyes of mocking groups of people. Nobody knew exactly how he made a living nowadays: a reporter, he sent articles to extreme-rightist newspapers in Belgium. He had been fired from several private schools, where he had persisted in preaching fascism and European revolution to the sons of nabobs of the automobile and pharmaceutical industries who had just flunked their *bac* in Lausanne. To subsist, he must have given some sort of private lessons at his home...

Mollendruz forced a smile.

"You're still at the Gymnase?"

Jean Calmet was horrified by that question.

"They still haven't fired me," he replied, without pleasure. It seemed to him that Mollendruz was soiling his students by making him talk about his work.

"Have you read our newspaper lately, Monsieur Calmet?"

Jean Calmet had not read it.

"That's odd," resumed Mollendruz. "We send it to all official buildings, and, what's more, each teacher gets his own copy at home. That's what you call information, don't you agree?"

He added with a fishy smile:

"We're forced to struggle against the leftist propaganda that barrages the teachers' room all day long..."

Jean Calmet listened to that language with amazement. The other man continued, screwing up his eyes, his hand trembling:

"There's just a handful of us, but I have confidence – our day will come! We can't let Europe go to ruin because of the undermining of irresponsible Maoists and anarchists who are governing under Nixon's protection. Just about everywhere, groups like ours are organizing or reorganizing. In Paris, in Brussels, in London and, of course, in Germany, people are reacting, people are becoming aware, they're arming, they're answering, they're taking a stand! No submitting any more, Monsieur Calmet! What we need is a core of determined men, militants who aren't afraid of violence. Remember the friends of Hitler and the SA in Munich when they organized their propaganda meetings in the beer halls. There were machine guns in the four corners of the hall, Monsieur Calmet; opposing parties were beaten unmercifully! They didn't waste any time! When I think that any little communist hooligan can get up and speak wherever he wants..."

In his excitement, the shrill voice rose in pitch, the little bat eyes gleamed in their ugly pink lining.

Had he been drinking? wondered Jean Calmet. No, it's his nerves, he believes everything that he's saying. I'm going to leave. I'm going to stand up, refuse to shake hands, walk out of this café! Awful guy. That is what Jean Calmet was thinking, but, nevertheless, he did not stand: oppressing confusion insinuated itself in him, began to weigh heavily, immobilized him under Mollendruz's gaze. The Lyrique was crowded, it was hot, the conversations and laughter had created a hubbub in which Jean Calmet was paralysed like an insect in birdlime. Mollendruz had fallen silent now. Jean Calmet lined up some coins on the table.

"Leaving so soon?" said Mollendruz with regret. "Really? Won't you come up to my place for a drink? Between colleagues... I live right nearby, you know. You haven't even let me pay for my round."

What was it about Mollendruz? Baseness? Jealousy towards a fellow teacher in the public-school system? A fear charged with emotion, above all, a shabby terror, a trembling at

159

the centre of his being that made him throw pink-eyed glances around him, quickly inspect the back of the café, spy on a neighbour, glance towards the glass partition of the telephone booth; then his eyes would come back to Jean Calmet and stare at him for a fraction of a second with a pitiable, interrogatory malice. That was it, all right. Mollendruz wondered if his act was going to work. A quarter to twelve. The café door was open on the rain, the waiters were asking people to pay their bills, the last customers put on their overcoats at the exit. Mollendruz persisted.

"Come on up to my place for a quick beer!"

Bad feeling. Embarrassment. Anger towards himself. But from a kind of unconscious mimicry that he was the first to despise in himself, Jean Calmet found himself unable to oppose Mollendruz, or even to leave him then and there. The other tagged along. They went out together.

"Really, I live right nearby," repeated Mollendruz in the cold rain. "Just a quick glass of beer…"

They climbed the Avenue Georgette. The last trolley buses were going back to the depot, their tyres splashing the pavement.

Two minutes. They reached Villamont.

"It's here," said Mollendruz, and he pushed open the door of a building, the ground floor of which was occupied by a florist's shop. As he went by, Jean Calmet noticed the horrible flesh-coloured hothouse cyclamens under the two floodlights of the shop window.

Mollendruz opened his door, turned on the light, pulled his guest by the arm to the threshold of an office and showed him in with ceremony.

"Look, Monsieur Calmet, look! All that must mean something to you, right?"

Jean Calmet stood there stunned, unable to move forward, while the sweat began running under his arms and on his brow.

At the back of the room, under a Third Reich flag topped by an eagle with outspread wings and the swastika, was a huge photograph of Hitler with an extraordinarily vivid expression. Then he saw a collection of trophies and decorations, among which he noticed military crosses, battalion flags, weapons, photographs, several insignia of principalities...

Mollendruz had put his hand on Jean Calmet's shoulder:

"Well, Monsieur Calmet, does my little museum astonish you? Look at that. Extremely rare. I know some people who'd give a fortune for that item."

And he spread out on the table a black armband edged with silver over which were traced Gothic letters of greyer silver:

SS – Schule Braunschweig

"One of the two schools of the Waffen SS, Monsieur Calmet. Think of that!"

And he caressed the black fabric, ran his fingers lovingly over the relief of the sharp-pointed letters, held out the armband to Jean Calmet, who shivered as if he had touched a snakeskin, and put it back on the small table hurriedly.

"The Waffen SS," mused Mollendruz. "Open that album, Monsieur Calmet!"

And he thrust into his hands a great bound notebook that was like an album of family photos: memories of parades, concerts, ceremonial parades by the glorious corps.

"But you came to drink a beer, Monsieur Calmet! I've forgotten you!"

He disappeared, the door of a refrigerator slammed; Jean Calmet heard Mollendruz handling bottles and glasses. He sat down in an armchair and waited. Embarrassed, perspiring, he could not escape the flaming of the red flag: in the centre of the crimson, in its circular area, the swastika revolved without stop, its nasty arms like the legs of an evil spider. Beneath it, gleaming in his black frame,

161

Adolf Hitler stared intensely in Jean Calmet's direction, as if he sought to speak to him beyond space and time, as if he sought to meet the eyes of the wretched man seated in one of his follower's armchairs, to convince him at any cost.

Mollendruz came back from the kitchen with bottles; he served the beer.

"Private chat with our Führer, eh, Monsieur Calmet? I agree with you one hundred per cent – that portrait has an astonishing forcefulness. He's alive! He's calling. Ah the pose of the bust, that erect silhouette, the fantastic power of the eyes!"

He added childishly, as if for himself:

"I don't know what I'd do without that photo…"

And in a louder voice:

"It was an authentic Nazi, one of the secretaries at the Kommandantur of Lyon, who gave it to me as a token of trust. Yes, the photo says it all right: our Führer isn't dead, Monsieur Calmet. Neither is the brilliant plan of the Great Reich, or the true Europe. Look at our symbol for what it is: the swastika. You see! It's alive! It doesn't stop turning, like the sun, like the earth, like the planets. It's the image of life, and nothing can stop it! What's more, it's a very simple sign: I've never gone into public urinals without finding graffiti of the swastika. Etched with the point of a pin, pencilled, scratched into the sheet metal – it doesn't matter, the symbol was there, beaming, radiating; it's proof that nothing can kill the cross of the Reich!"

Then a surprising thing happened. Mollendruz set his glass of beer on the little table and marched briskly up to Hitler's portrait. Two yards from the photograph he stopped, froze, clicked his heels with violence and raised his arm:

"*Heil Hitler!*"

He had barked in the silence of the sleeping house.

Jean Calmet had given a start, but Mollendruz did not give him the time to recover. He turned around to his guest, an expression of defiance in his small, hooded eyes:

"We'll win, Monsieur Calmet. We'll take back Europe, we'll reconquer the whole world!"

He was moving like a mannequin. "And what am I doing here?" Jean Calmet said to himself bitterly. "I'm dumbfounded, and this comedy is making me sick." He had lost any notion of time. He drank his beer mechanically. He had forgotten Thérèse, and his students, and his lessons; he was sinking into a viscous insipidity. The beer was sticky. His glass was sticky. Nevertheless, he let himself go on drinking without stop, his stomach heavy.

Nearly another hour went by, during which Mollendruz, overexcited, had Jean Calmet leaf through a stack of *Gringoire* and *Je suis partout* and study in detail a board where Jewish profiles, noses, mouths, earlobes, hairlines, shoulders, bellies, soles of feet were categorized and commented on at length under a heading in big capitals:

LEARN TO RECOGNIZE THE KIKES!

Nausea burned his stomach. He got to his feet suddenly, furious, desperate. He did not have to shake Mollendruz's hand; the latter already understood that he had gone too far. Mollendruz stood, motionless, on the threshold, somewhat bent; only his eyes searched Jean Calmet's face with obvious satisfaction. Jean Calmet gave him a nod, started down the staircase, went out into the cold air.

It was no longer raining. Three hours to sleep. All the humiliation of that evening on his shoulders, Jean Calmet climbed back up Villamont with the sad thought that, of the Gymnase's faculty, he was indeed the only one to be on the street at that hour, and to come away from such an ignoble encounter. And the rest of that short night, to punish him, his father came back in his dreams: there was the bull charging down from the top of the black hill and smashing him, there was the study in Lutry, the doctor strangling him in his ogreish arms before the tall clock like a coffin standing on end. And at dawn, while the blackbirds were already singing in the gardens, someone shouted "*Heil Hitler!*" at the back of a courtyard, and woke Jean Calmet from his fever.

While shaving, his eyes following the progress of the blade over his skin, he was still belching the beer that he had not had time to digest.

The big blue trolley bus came onto the Place Saint-François by the feeding lane on the right. Jean Calmet had stopped in the sun before the shop window of Manuel, the caterer. All of a sudden, a rat came out of a cellar ventilator almost beside him and began to zigzag, panic-stricken, over the pavement. A fraction of a second! Jean Calmet had only had the time to think: A rat! – then he would say to himself that it was a big grey rat, with a hairless back, with a long pink tail, and he would believe that he had even registered the sound of the little claws on the pavement – already the rat has hurled itself into the bright light; dazzled, it runs without seeing anything, the blue trolley bus comes abreast of the church, accelerating to make the green light on the Grand-Pont, the rat dashes out. No, no, Jean Calmet thinks foolishly. The rat and the trolley bus must necessarily meet. There, it's done, the huge right wheel has bitten into a rat's round, tapering body; the eight yards of the vehicle roll on past before Jean Calmet, who does not move, who looks; in the sun there is a patch of gleaming red between the cars, which slow down and stop in line.

Jean Calmet went up to the patch.

The rat had burst under the weight.

Up close, he saw that there were two different sets of remains. The first, the one that he had seen from the pavement, that was the rat's envelope, the skin which was still stuck to the completely flattened skull. A red shape, outlined exactly, the tail attached to the burst bag, the head flat as crimson leaf; in the muzzle there are still two little teeth plainly visible, curved, childlike in the dust. The whole profile is an oily red that is already taking on the metallic reflections of the coagulating blood.

The other set of remains was a bundle of pink and green viscera which had spurted two yards when the bag had burst.

Three o'clock in the afternoon.

Jean Calmet had a date with Thérèse.

He climbed back up the Rue de Bourg thinking about the rat's martyrdom. For years, the animal had dwelt in the cellars and recesses under the fashionable boutiques. The fine shoe stores, the glittering jewellery shops; for years it had roamed, ferreted, made up inventories, surveyed its labyrinth under the richest elegance of Europe. Under the stocks of minks and the rivers of diamonds. Under the loads of caviar. Under the rubies, the carats, the electronic watches, the narcissistic clock-maker's shops. Under the *box-calf* and hand-sewn ankle boots. One afternoon, towards twenty minutes to three, it had come out of its lair. Chance? Pushed out by a stroke of fate? Driven out by the other rats? Boredom? Whim? Desire to see the world? It had had enough of its wildness; it had gone out into the sun and it had been squashed four yards further on. One is not safe being independent in our part of the world. Not safe staying wild and uncompromising in the city. Jean Calmet remembered the porcupine that had given him advice one moonlit night, the cat that he had followed along the lake. They, too, were *francs-tireurs*, madmen, hermits, panic-stricken ones. For two years, three years, the rat had lived, had defied the city, proud, violent, wrapped up in its appetites and its desires, watchful plunderer, a lord hemmed in and silent under the centre of town, lonely brain that ran like a little lamp in the corridors of shadow, underground heart beneath the public heart, beneath the noisy heart in broad daylight!

Jean Calmet reached the top of the Rue de Bourg; he turned left, crossed Saint-Pierre and started over the Bessières bridge, which spans, high up, the Rue Saint-Martin. It was the bridge of suicides: several times a week, people leapt out into space and crashed thirty yards below in front of the pumps of the Peugeot garage. The filling-station attendant kept a sack of sawdust within reach to sop up the puddle of blood, in which his customers' cars might skid and be spattered. Without waiting for the city ambulance to get there, the attendant, by tradition, covered the smashed body: that blanket could be seen, at all times, carefully folded next to one of the gas pumps. It was spotted and appeared to be hardened with brown crusts.

Crossing the bridge, Jean Calmet kept as far as possible from the guard rail because of vertigo, and he would imagine, each time, the whole delirious mechanism of the condemned person's last seconds. I stop on the pavement; I grip the railing firmly in my hands; I swing my leg over the metal bar; now I see the street below, the garage, the dazzling pavement at the bottom of the abyss; I don't hesitate; I want to die; I don't hesitate; I heave my body; Christ, I'm in space, I'm falling, breath taken away... I... Jean Calmet had heard people say that the fall made you lose consciousness before you hit the ground.

Horror.

Middle of the bridge.

Those who threw themselves off here were also wild, eager, silent ones whom the world had fenced off and put to death.

Like the rat. Like all those heroic animals that were fighting against the concrete, the hydrocarbons, vanity, superstition, mindless pleasure, baseness: hawks gunned down at high noon, foxes tracked down with gas, badgers clubbed to death in the snare, screech owls crucified, mice drowned in their traps, bullfinches pierced with compressed-air rifles, squirrels poisoned with strychnine, fawns with legs cut by mechanical reapers, wild boar machine-gunned in their sleep, hares strangled, deer shot with automatic rifles, cats used as targets by the midnight hit-and-run drivers, toads, frogs, porcupines of the back roads like bloody omelettes under the cool breeze... Thérèse was waiting for him at the Café de l'Évêché.

What mystery in her. Like a soft fruit, and the skin too is mysterious, she gleams gently; there is a light from her hair that illuminates her beautiful face bent over a book, her big forehead, the flawless cheekbones, the neck, where an iron necklace runs down, disappearing into the embroidered blouse. She has her jeans, wooden clogs. A girl. She will be twenty on 16 August. The sign of Leo. In the white linen, under a band of old-fashioned embroidery, her bosom makes two spheres. Jean Calmet would like to open her collar, free one breast, fasten his mouth to the aureole and suck, suck life at that spring, bury himself once and for all in the maternal sweetness.

She raised her eyes.

Two green fountains.

She smiled, her teeth shone for a second, she set the book on the table. It was *The Lily of the Valley*.

Standing, Jean Calmet looked at her.

"Want to go for a walk in La Cité?" she asked.

They went behind the cathedral, walked along the level ground where, the autumn before, Jean Calmet had seen one of his students lean over the skeleton of a monk and put a flower between the teeth.

Thérèse went barefoot in big wooden clogs painted white; her steps rang out gaily in the little streets, deserted at that hour of the afternoon, and Jean Calmet marvelled once more that this girl was so strangely close to childhood, fairy tales, scenes etched on copper in the old books with pink covers, plates spotted with freckles, which the booksellers and antique dealers display in their front windows, hung up with clothespins. As if the clack-clack of those clogs had been enough to bring back a whole past of young marvels in which Jean Calmet recognized the power of Thérèse: his girls, his sisters, his little cousins of the hearth and the woods, and the dwarfs, the fairies, the sorcery, the animals starting to speak at the banks of rivers, girls awakened from death by a kiss, wives shut up in the red room while the road is smothered in dust and the grass turns green on the immense fields up to the foot of the Jura, where the night comes.

That is what struck him about her the first time that he saw her at the Café de l'Évêché. That mixture of freshness and very old wisdom. The cradle part and the cat part. The candour and the suppleness. The blond, the nocturnal. The spirit of fairies, and I who wasn't able to love you! Couldn't. Couldn't. The clogs clack against the pavement, it is a distinct, sweet sound, a rather loud one; all of a sudden the giants gesticulate, the little boy strews his bread in the deep woods, and already the birds are watching the light-coloured crumbs from high up in their branches. Clack-clack. Ironic clogs, they laugh, they make their happy sound, they are mocking, couldn't, coo-coo, clack the wooden shoes, poor old fool, I'm young, I'm twenty, I come, I go, I have fun, I cry, I make love with Marc, I draw cats, I lick ice cream, I drop out of the Beaux-Arts, I go back there, I have my mother in Montreux, I don't give a damn, the sun is falling red behind the bandstand. And I have very pretty round breasts that soon become eager under Marc's

168

tongue. And I have a little basket. Long-waisted, as they say in the fashion catalogues. Jean? Monsieur Calmet? I loved him for two or three days. He's deep. I understand him without understanding him. He never talks about himself. He has eyes that tell too much about him. One afternoon, he screamed in a café. I took him to my place. I felt like making love. It didn't work. Since then he's been looking at me with even wilder eyes. Marc told me that one day he talked to him about his father: an odd sort of fellow, his father, as strange as he is, a little on the brutal side. An intelligent brute, apparently dangerous. I have my mother in Montreux, and Papa had the good idea of dying at high noon on a glacier. Jean used to call me the Cat Girl. Maybe because I have a little pussy that's sweet and warm and wet. Maybe because I do as I please. I betrayed him. Is the word too strong? I love Marc. Too bad about Jean. I don't want to make him suffer. He can come to my room as long as he likes. I won't back out…

But it isn't that simple, and he knows it. But this is the way Jean Calmet tortured himself along the old streets of La Cité one summer afternoon, when the roses weighed heavily on the trelliswork of the Place de la Barre and the blackbirds were calling in the chestnut trees. He hurt himself all along the alleys; the music of the wooden clogs ended up obsessing him; the fairy beside him was humming and picking carnations in the old walls, marvelling at their vanilla odour. She slipped the flowers into her basket. Another souvenir of the fairy tales, when the highwayman watches from behind the brambles and puts on a pleasant face for going up to the little girl.

Four o'clock. No breeze. It was stifling. A heavy, humid heat. It's the time when one would like to get off the street, shut oneself up in the back room of a café, climb a staircase at random, stretch out in a cool room. The hour of the wolf, the doctor used to say, in Lutry, peering into the little boy's eyes. The brick-red mug loomed before Jean Calmet, set in its cruelty. I'm made for suffering, he thought to himself while walking. Chopped meat. Flesh to be nailed. Childhood? Washed away. The rest smashed. My father, Liliane, Thérèse... There are only the prostitutes, fat Pernette, and it's even worse afterwards. And Mother? He was ashamed, thinking about food immediately, about that old mouth that made its lonely noise in the deserted dining room, and, outside, the sun sinks over the lake, the blood of the evening falls on the floor, Mother is alone, Mother is going to die, oh in two years, in three years, she's trembling more and more, she's been broken since Papa's death, she waits for a phone call all day, she talks to herself, she keeps sitting before the window for hours, and the dusk lights up her poor wrinkled face, she remembers, she stares into space...

The sky became grey, blackish; suddenly it was purple, and the thunder split, a silvery rain fell violently over the city, ripping the leaves off the trees, hurling itself in torrents over the slopes of La Cité. Thérèse ran ahead of Jean Calmet, her clogs in her hand, turning back to smile at him. They came to her doorway.

"Come on in and dry out," she said, and Jean Calmet saw once again the narrow corridor, the small landing, the card pinned on the door:

Thérèse Dubois
Étudiante

Right away she was close to him, her face uplifted, her green-fountain eyes planted in his gaze, and for a few seconds Jean Calmet knew her sweetness again. By the kind of rift that opened up within him he knew that her mysteriousness was at work, filling in the wound with forests, cats, birds, magic roads at dawn, villages glimpsed on emerald hills, lucernes in the white light where the wind shifts. Thérèse drew closer still, he had her wet hair right against his mouth, he put his lips on her forehead where the tepid rain trickled.

For a moment they remained motionless, silent. They were standing before the open window, and the storm was still cracking over the gleaming rooftops of the Gymnase.

Then she broke away, closed the window and unbuttoned her blouse:

"A shower," she said. "I'm freezing!"

Jean Calmet could never get used to that haste. In a moment, her clothes had been rolled up into a ball and tossed into a corner of the room; naked and lithe, she came into view, she ran to the bathroom, the water began spraying.

"Jean! Come scrub my back – I'm cold!"

Thérèse sitting in the bathtub.

Hair, hair, open over her shoulder; all that gold, which reddens under the shower; her back arches, offers itself to the stream.

Jean Calmet sat on the rim of the bathtub.

"Soap me," said Thérèse.

She looks like a little girl, she showers her shoulders, she puts the flexible nozzle down at the bottom of the water. She lies down, stretches her legs out, sits up again, wedges her back against the head of the bathtub, brings her knees together, watches Jean Calmet with a questioning look.

Jean Calmet is afraid. And what if his father were going to watch him? If the Ogre's eye killed him on the spot? He would take Thérèse. Annihilating him, his youngest; and his bursts of laughter resounded in Jean Calmet's ears.

He nevertheless took the bar of soap and ran it over the fairy's neck, his hand touches her muscles, squeezes them, his fingers follow her collarbones, climb back up to the smooth throat.

Lyre of her shoulders.

Hiding place of her armpits.

Circuit of her arms, up to the wrists that are extended, return to the curly armpits, to the collarbones, very gentle road to the nape of the neck, on the way he spreads her hair, he caresses the down under the rain of gold, he touches her vertebrae with his fingernails, Thérèse shakes herself, he returns to the pale, slender neck.

Solidity of that neck.

Fragility of the collarbones.

Resistance of her breasts under his hand. His palm insists, goes around it quickly, his thumb crushes the aureole, goes away, his hand takes the lithe apple again, squeezes, its roundness does not come undone.

His hand descends, explores the curve of her hips.

Her belly is lifted, offering itself like a basket of marvels. Navel full of soap suds. Pubis all white: a carnation that shines. Length of her legs, toes that Jean Calmet counts and re-counts like jacks, like the beads of a smooth, warm rosary, my daughter, my little girl, I love you oh my tenderness, oh my child, I'll finger your pink nails, Tom Thumb, I'll strew your toes in the forest, thanks to you I'll find my way...

Then Jean Calmet dried her in a big red towel.

Then he combed her long hair that was dripping.

Then he set the blower on "warm air", and he was surprised to see her hair, lank and dark from the water, regain its suppleness and its gold as the blower ran.

Then he put the blower on "cool air" and caressed her head, her neck for a long time, from close up, from further away, going back down over the nape of her neck, touching her shoulders with the cool wind, returning to the temples, the forehead, sculpting her hair, which fled and curved under the jet of air, ascending once more to the top of her skull, my Melusina, my Ophelia, finding again the light-coloured furrow between her shoulders covered with golden down, playing at hunting the golden tuft which fled immediately before the barrel of the blower, making her hips shudder, turning about her breasts which goosefleshed at once, lingering at the wide, brown aureoles, which shrank and were covered with hard little grains. And what did Jean Calmet feel during these games? He saw Thérèse grow excited, and a kind of exasperation seized him at rousing that silken body without his own desire being whetted for a second. First he had seen his father considering him with an ironic look: "You're trying to arouse yourself, Jean Calmet. You know very well that it's impossible. They're for me, those dainty morsels. Leave that girl alone. You know you'll never be able to have her." And the doctor laughed on the threshold of the room. Nevertheless, Jean Calmet continued, he persevered, and he was aware of devising more and more exciting caresses as he felt the shame overwhelm him. Impotent, he said to himself, I'm setting that fruit ablaze, and I stay paralysed. The humiliation brought tears to his eyes. The blower pursued an imaginary enemy between the shoulder blades of Thérèse, who bent to experience the whole caress more completely: stooping that way, breathing fast, yielding, taut with desire, she was extraordinarily beautiful, and Jean hated himself with violence. My father wouldn't let this prey go by. He cursed himself cruelly. He imagined the old man's erect penis, the knotty stick, the big purple glans lunging towards the adorable fleshy fruit; the penis drew close, greedy, aiming at the pink antrum, entering it, provoking cries and sobs of joy...

Thérèse was panting softly.

"Jean, come into my bed, come next to me, Jean," she said; and pressing herself against him, she crushed her breasts on his chest, she clasped her hands around his neck, she drew his head to her, taking his mouth in her mouth.

Despondent, Jean Calmet allowed himself to be drawn towards the bed, allowed himself to be laid down on his back like a child. He had his eyes closed, heinous humiliation gripped his throat. Stomach knotted. Nausea. Rage. My father had Liliane sent to him, I surprised them, she was naked in front of the window, he was feeling her breasts... She touched, she gathered, she sucked the doctor's huge swollen glans. Jean Calmet was choking with pain and sadness. Impotent. In the doorway his father was roaring with laughter.

"Benjamin! Get ready! Now's the time to show what you can do!"

Now Thérèse undressed him with tender precision. Unbuttoned his shirt, removed it, Jean Calmet felt her quick fingers on his skin; then a hand unbuckled his belt, opened his trousers, ran to his hips, came back to his belly, slid itself under his briefs... Heinously, Jean Calmet broke away from the embrace. He got up, pulled his shirt back on, buckled his belt, left the room without looking at the bed, slammed the door. That's the last time. I'll never see her again, he thought as he went down the stairs. Never again. Never again. Sobs of shame and despair rose in his throat. He found himself on the street, like a ghost. Night was falling. It was no longer raining; from the yard of the Gymnase the smell of clean earth and wet leaves rose, breaking his heart.

Jean Calmet walked down the street, went around the cathedral and started across the Bessières bridge. He walked head down, ruminating over his chagrin. Suddenly, lifting his eyes, he saw Bloch, a schoolmate from his secondary school, Jacques Bloch, the pharmacist, who was coming the other way on the same pavement. A few yards away, Bloch smiled at him and greeted him when they passed.

"Dirty Jew!" said Jean Calmet loud enough to be heard. Sneering, he took a few more steps, then repeated clearly:

"Dirty Jew!"

Then he went close to the guard rail of the bridge, and he looked into the abyss. The vertigo and all his baseness gave him a stinking nausea. For a long time he vomited bile on the toes of his shoes.

Three days before his death – it was Friday 15 June – Jean Calmet woke up very early and remembered the night before with horror. Of course he did not know that he was going to die, and he believed that he was going to make the same movements, suffer the same sights, love them, and do his work like any other day.

He went down to the Gymnase on foot and stopped at the Café de l'Évêché, where he ordered a cup of coffee. As he was about to pay, he toyed with a five-franc piece on the table, and suddenly he stared at it with exasperated attention. There was something there, at least, that he had not seen before! On the face of the big, solid coin, the man personifying Switzerland had a calm strength and self-assurance that wounded him immediately. He was seen in profile: a great untroubled forehead, strong, regular nose, thin mouth, resolute chin. Then the garment opened on a muscular throat and torso; his head, some curly hair of which could be seen, bore the hood of the peasants of old Switzerland that they are always shown wearing – threshers, hunters, woodsmen just and strong in their faith alone. But the man was clean-shaven, so he eluded the William Tell image and approached our century. And the weight of the metal, the long inscription crowning the character: CONFOEDERATIO HELVETICA; the worn beauty of the man and the regularity of his features gave him serene power that aggravated Jean Calmet's loneliness.

He paid in a violent temper and threw the change into his jacket pocket.

CONFOEDERATIO HELVETICA. He was going to give a Latin lesson. The man's profile seemed to sneer at him. Why did he repeat over and over that inscription, which was so insolent in its calm simplicity? Of course, he realized with fright, Latin was the paternal language. The sacred language, the language of power and the indestructible. And he, Jean Calmet, would soon be reading Latin, and translating, and annotating, and redistributing Latin. Woodlouse, slug, he would crawl over the eternal monument, he was going to drag his vile legs, his mandibles, his scales, his drool over the hallowed stone! Who are you, Jean Calmet, to dare insult your father's resting place? Do you think you will ever enter it? It resists all attack! It fights back! The stronghold towers over you! From the height of its age, from the depth of its vigour, it looks at you and sees at its foot your miserable insect's stature, which does its utmost to nibble the skin of its stones!

Overwhelmed, Jean Calmet listened to the hideous voice thunder in his ears. Master of Latin! – Latin master? Aren't you ashamed, Jean Calmet, you, the weakling, to dare cling to my authority? You're dirty. You're short of breath. And for years you've dared to defile my walls. Appropriate fragments of my house. The language of your father, Jean Calmet! You won't set foot there any more! You don't have the right, you hear. That language belongs to the strong. It belongs to the powerful men of the earth!

Jean Calmet had stopped. Groups of students dressed in bright colours were going past him, chatting in very loud tones. He turned around: thirty yards away came François Clerc. Talk to him? Ask him for help? What good would it do? François Clerc had never known terror. He wouldn't understand. He taught his classes, he created, he was generous and strong. Jean Calmet started walking again, and when he reached the small square near the cathedral, instead of going to the Gymnase, he scurried to the right and sheltered himself for a few moments in the hall of the film library.

I can't. I can't go there, he thought. It's Virgil this morning, a third-year class. I can't.

He came back out, quickly assured himself that nobody had seen him, ran to the Pomme de Pin, and, from the bistro, telephoned the Gymnase to say he was sick that morning, that he would undoubtedly be absent on Saturday as well, that he would be back on Monday without fail. Madame Oisel told him again that the written part of the *bac* began on Monday at eight o'clock and that, several weeks before, he had been designated invigilator for one of the classes. Jean Calmet promised and hung up.

He was free. He started to breathe again.

All of a sudden, he had to assure himself that the doctor's ashes were still shut up behind the iron gate of the columbarium.

He's dead all right, that bastard, he thought. A little heap of ashes. I'm not going to let myself be pushed around by that bag of dust. And, along the sunlit streets, he made his way down to the crematorium.

The ivy shone on the old walls. Jean Calmet started into the tree-lined lane. Sparrows fluttered over lawns. Blackbirds hopped among the beds of iris and roses. Jean Calmet stopped and looked at them. When he started on his way again, a stream of water showered him as he went by, and more sparrows, quick and odd, were bathing their wings in the glistening water.

Silhouetted at the end of the path rose the chimney of the crematorium.

Jean climbed the steps of a staircase, on the right, and the columbarium appeared. He went up to it. The iron gate was closed. At first, completely dazzled, he could only make out vague forms in the shadows. Then he saw it: at the back of its niche stood the great urn of shelly marble. Stopping, gluing his eye to the metal, Jean Calmet could read with certainty:

DOCTEUR PAUL CALMET
1894–1972

Good. From that standpoint, there was peace. But what if the voice attacked him again? If the eye searched his heart? The urn was locked behind that iron gate, but it seemed that the doctor was in the air, sly, infallible, and even more mobile in death. His words thundered in Jean Calmet's skull and resounded in his dreams. His gaze pierced his brain, oppressed his movements, laughed at his most carefully hidden plans. Devoured alive, Jean Calmet. He made a gesture of weariness and turned aside towards the garden. The sun was already white, the heat rose… He crossed the cemetery again and was out on the street once more.

Then, as he wanted to take a census of his family in a useless, desperate album, he hailed a taxi and went down to the door of Les Peupliers. He did not go in right away. He walked around the house, reached the lake by the orchard, climbed back up along the line of laurel trees. The downstairs windows were open. Above him, to the right, under the roof, the shutters of his room were closed. All the better. The doctor's eyes had finished piercing walls. Jean Calmet saw himself once more, exhausted, in the shadows, pretending to read, expecting – from one minute to the next – the Ogre's gaze or voice to pull him from his hiding place and throw him back into the circus. But the shutters of the study were closed too, and he felt a glad satisfaction that gave him new courage. He reached the front door and rang. His mother opened it and beamed.

"Jean, it's you, Jean, my baby. Then you're off today?"

Jean Calmet did not answer. He kissed his mother, he went into the vestibule and recognized at once the smell of his childhood: the consulting room and the cellar. The disinfectant, the doctors, and those musty smells of winter apples that rose from the basement. He turned around to the old woman and took her in his arms: a little bundle of deformed bones, the pallid face of a clown, the wrinkled brow, pink at the temples, where the carefully drawn locks of hair revealed the frayed skin...

The dining room was all lit up by the eleven o'clock sun. The long pendulum of the clock beat in the glass-doored case. The table gleamed. On the wall, the earthenware was perfectly shiny, and in front of the window, on the armchair, he could see a piece of embroidery that his mother had dropped at the sound of the doorbell. She's fighting, thought Jean Calmet. She's trying to fight back. Loneliness, old age, nothing stops her. She's bent with age, she can't sleep any more, but still she runs her house, she works, she eats every day. I'm sure she carries her meal to the big table. She has fought back all her life, in her own way, without saying a word, apparently resigned; and perhaps it's propriety? Or pride? She doesn't ask anyone for help... With tenderness he looked at that tidiness, the sewing left unfinished on the armchair, and when the old woman sat down again, he pulled a chair next to her and gently took her hand.

"You see, I keep busy, but I get tired right away..."

The veins in her hands stood out, periwinkle blue, the arthritis obliterated her wrinkled skin and the wrist that was all knotted. Now they talked about him; about his work, about the Gymnase. She gave him news of his brothers and sisters. She had received a visit from the pastor. She was only going to services one Sunday a month...

Jean Calmet looked at photos of his nephews: she had just received them, she tried to find resemblances, bring back memories, spoke of the orchard where nobody had gathered the cherries, she planned – that autumn – to give the crop of apples to the hospital.

"Since nobody eats them…" she said pensively.

And lifting her eyes to Jean Calmet:

"My youngest child," she said, and her grey eyes, her washed-out eyes, her worn eyes peered anxiously into her son's eyes.

Jean Calmet turned his head away and got to his feet. He took a few steps, looked at the clock as if he were seeing it for the first time, studied the wood, the dial, the mechanism, which he could see under the enamel through a rectangular opening.

He reached the floor above, opened the door of his room, but did not switch on the light. At the back of the room, vaguely illuminated by the light from the hallway, he saw his childhood bed, a table, a little bookcase, where there were still a few of his books from those days. He went past his brothers' doors, past the room where both his sisters had slept. He opened that door, and a sickish feeling gripped him: what was he looking for among these ghosts? Cries, sobs, laughter rang out on the deserted landing. At the back of his sisters' room, dolls gleamed weakly. Ill at ease, he switched off the light, the dolls disappeared; he closed the door again without a sound. He went past the study door – "CONSULTATIONS every day from 1 to 7 p.m. except Thursday" – almost entered, retraced his steps, went back to his mother, who had not moved.

He bent over her and gave her a quick kiss on the forehead. She got to her feet to accompany him. Was she going to suggest that he stay for the meal? She did not dare. She remained silent. She mumbled a goodbye; Jean Calmet wished her well, took her hand again and placed a kiss on it. She walked him to the door:

"Come back soon!"

He took the trolley bus and went back up to the Rovéréaz without stopping in a café and without daring to go back out, for fear of being seen by a student or by someone from the secretary's office.

Two days before his death, Jean Calmet still did not know what was going to happen to him. That was Saturday 16 June. He woke up early as usual, but, on that morning, the thought of the duty that he had to perform pushed him to his table right away, and he opened the telephone directory.

The idea had come to him the night before, between two dreams: he had to write to Bloch. He had to explain Mollendruz to him. Tell him the story. Hide nothing from him about the confusion of the last few weeks; he would understand, he would excuse, so this shame would be washed away; Jean Calmet had not ceased to suffer at the thought of the ignoble words.

He took an envelope and wrote the address in longhand:

> *Monsieur Jacques Bloch*
> *Pharmacist*
> *7, Avenue du Théâtre*
> *1005 Lausanne*

Then he began his letter.

My dear Bloch,

he wrote. But the words did not please him. *Dear,* after the other night's insult? Bloch would tear the letter up as soon as he opened it! No, Bloch was good. Bloch knew. He had

181

to trust Bloch. He was an old classmate from school, after all, he would not be able to refuse the clear explanation being given to him.

Jean Calmet read the letter over and began to write again.

> *My dear Bloch,*
> *You were doubtless astonished the night before last, on the Bessières bridge*

and then he stopped again... *Astonished*... Actually that was putting it mildly. People had been insulting Bloch for four thousand years. His cousins from Poland had ended up in ovens. In Paris, his grandfather had worn the yellow star. *Astonished?* It would be burning him again, torturing him, deporting him, annihilating all of his children, all of his race. Speak to him about Mollendruz? What did Mollendruz have to do with it? Jean Calmet was the louse. He was the one who had been unable to withstand a few hours of stupidity. He was the one whose sleep Hitler's photograph had returned to haunt. He was the one who thought of avenging his humiliation by degrading the first person he passed after running from Thérèse's place. He was the miserable one who had begun to be violently anti-Semitic because he was enraged by his weakness. Oven-ogre, thought Jean Calmet. Mengele-ogre. Mollendruz bat-ogre. Spineless vampire. Jean Calmet-ogre. And out of revenge. What baseness.

He took up the pen again and forced himself to continue:

> *...on the Bessières bridge, to hear me call you...*

No, it was impossible. He was not going to write rubbish like that. He had to make it shorter. Not remind him of anything. Send a word, a *cri du cœur*, Bloch will be able to read between the lines. He will see that I am wretched. I wasn't aiming at you, Jacques Bloch – I was after myself. I'll write this afternoon. I'll tear up the sheet of paper and put the envelope in plain sight on the desk. He even stuck a stamp on it, but he did not know that the letter would never be written and that the envelope would wind up under the seals of the magistrate, with its neat rubber stamp, between the Latin papers and the latest circulars to teachers of ancient languages at the Gymnase.

In the afternoon, which was traditionally free, he went down into town and went to Monsieur Liechti's for a shave. He enjoyed stretching out in the barber's chair, being soaped at length, feeling the blade run over his skin, crackling.

He did not write to Bloch. He roamed in the alleys of La Palud.

Going past La Louve, he debated over going up to Pernette's place and abandoned the idea: she must have her Saturday clients, Italians, Spaniards; he felt unwelcome, he continued wandering, but, for several hours, he missed the shiny fat flesh and the lipstick that tasted of grenadine. At a stand on the Place Centrale, he bought a pocket book of the *Satyricon* and threw it down a sewer one hundred yards further on. He had just reminded himself that he did not have the right to defile Latin. He did not feel like struggling to convince himself of the contrary.

He went back home.

He was worn out from his wandering in the streets. He was trembling in the heat. He went to bed early.

That night he had no dreams, at least he thought not, and he rested completely.

The following day, which was Sunday 17 June, Jean Calmet masturbated on waking, and when he had had his meagre pleasure, he remembered the jokes of his comrades in the military: "It's easier than screwing a woman. You don't need

a real hard-on. And, at any rate, there's less machinery."
Laughter. But they had women. Disgust. His fingers sticky,
Jean Calmet got to the bathroom and looked at himself
furtively in the mirror. He went back to bed.

Fell asleep again.

When he awoke, church bells were ringing, and he imagined the groups of worshippers waiting on the square
in front of the church, the robed pastor coming out of
the vestry and slowly climbing the steps of the pulpit, the
cold nave where the chants rose. He spent the day doing
nothing. Should I write to Bloch? I'll do it tomorrow. Nor
did he write to Thérèse, as he had vaguely intended to do.

With her, all is lost. What good is it to explain to her what
I couldn't tell her by loving her? Then he began wishing
that he could see her again by chance on the road to the
Gymnase. Would he greet her? Yes, she would come towards
him, there would be trees streaming with light, the wind,
the blue of the sky over the rooftops and a pavement café to
sit in and drink beer. They would be friends. The summer
would be long. And this autumn, when classes resumed,
he would look at the world with clear eyes.

The day of his death, which was Monday 18 June, Jean
Calmet did not get up. Obviously, he could not know that
his last day had come. Nevertheless, there were signs that
morning which a shrewder or less uncertain man would
not have failed to interpret more clearly.

For example, he did not telephone the Gymnase, and
for someone as conscientious, that error of judgement,
under ordinary circumstances, would have been the worst
kind of foolishness.

Half-past six. He was lying flat in his bed, he felt weary, he
was daydreaming. What was he going to do with the morning? Nothing, really, he would do nothing. Would he call
in just the same? He did not have the strength. Impossible.

The taste of dirty saliva. A phosphorescent fatigue as after a long night march.

Had he dreamt? He did not remember anything. No nightmare. No fever. A white slime.

He took his penis in his right hand, thinking about his comrades in the military. Easier than machinery.

But no shame this time.

Mentholated tissue.

Half sleep.

A little later, Jean Calmet did not dress himself. He stayed in pyjamas, grey ones with blue stripes, made of nylon, that his mother had given him for Christmas. He walked in pyjamas from one room to the other, barefoot, casting on his books and papers a gaze that conveyed nothing.

He had opened the blinds, and the gardens of Rovéréaz sent a green light into the apartment. It was half-past seven. People were hurrying towards the city. Jean Calmet did not stir. Another sign. For several long minutes, he stayed before a window watching leaves and birds move in a hedge of hazel bushes at the end of the gravel at the entrance. Then he sat down at his desk and shifted ballpoint pens on a blotter.

It was eight o'clock when he went into the bathroom. He opened his razor.

The blade shone on the metal head. He lifted it off, closed the razor again, put it back in its blue case.

He took the blade and lay down again on his bed.

For a moment, he looked at it in the light, his hand outstretched. Against the light, it made a rectangular sil-houette whose sharp edges gleamed. He therefore acts quickly, with surprising decisiveness for someone who has been lying about for days.

Holding the blade firmly between the thumb and index finger of his right hand, he pressed it against his left wrist, and, with the edge, he gently caressed the tendons and the main artery an inch from his hand. The blade was very keen. Jean Calmet felt the edge cut the skin; he shivered in spite of himself and looked at his forearm: a little red line was filling up with blood where the blade had gone. He did not put it down on the bedside table, as he had a terrible desire to do.

It was then that the die was cast.

All of a sudden, with an extraordinary force that he concentrated on that single point, he pressed on the blade, drove it into his left wrist and slowly sliced the radial artery and the flesh. Next, the right wrist...

He carefully placed the bloody blade on the little table next to the lamp and some books.

To his great surprise, the blood had not spurted. It oozed, tepid, thick; it was like a suction that tickled him over the slight smarting of the two wounds. He noticed that he was not thinking: for a minute, he had been making moves whose precision had absorbed him. He applied himself. The blood was not running fast enough, he had to help it. He let both his arms hang out over the side of his bed and he lay there, his arms outspread, motionless, while two scarlet streams trickled from his wrists into his palms and dripped from his fingers.

Jean Calmet waited, and now his thoughts were rushing with sharp clarity. He was not suffering. It was a crossing, a passage, where he shivered as in a dark trough. Faces, places appeared: the brown face of a girl glimpsed in a café, she was knitting, on her neck she had Arab jewellery made of plaited iron. Verret prostrated in the teachers' room. A porcupine with shining nose in the moonlight. The orchard in Lutry, a slow-worm had been cut in two by a scythe, the two coppery sections wriggled in the sun...

His thoughts returned to his wrists. The blood was hardly running any more. It was beginning to coagulate, no doubt because of the dry air on that summer morning, and Jean

Calmet remembered that he had to dip his arms into hot water to promote the drainage.

When he arose, the two red streams were seeping again; he was pleased by this, but he noticed with disgust that the blood had already made two little gluey pools on the floor, and he wondered who would clean them up sooner or later. A malaise seized him. He wondered if he could walk. A black wing, painful, crossed his brain like a migraine; pincers bit into him above the elbow and at the thighs.

His wrists extended in front of him, he reached the bathroom and knelt before the bathtub. The blood had stained the sleeves of the pyjamas. Jean Calmet rolled them up and turned on the hot water. Drops of blood fell on the enamel and spread out in stars on the perfect white. The faucet made an infernal din: Jean Calmet reduced the volume and stuck his wrists under the water. Now the blood was spurting. The entire bathtub was spattered with red. He had to make a mighty effort to remain on his knees, his trunk erect, his arms extended, while the faucet continued to drill through his skull, and all kinds of noises struck him like echoes of the horrible din: the lake assailing the breakwater at Lutry, the stormy nights, the bells of the old town, the fountain in the small square of the Grand Council, where the pigeons go to drink and bathe in the evening, and the scraping of chairs and the laughter lull to sleep the heart and the memory more surely than the weariness at the close of the day. But he was growing drowsy, too. He was aware of beginning to bend towards the whiteness of the enamel covered with crimson seals; try as he might to straighten up by fits and starts, he would fall forward again, and his arms, still extended, weighed him down now like intolerable burdens. For some time he had not felt the sizzling of the water at his wrists. Had not felt the blood escaping from him. He closed his eyes. He was going to sleep. Gently. To sleep.

He was on the verge of losing consciousness, and he caught himself on the rim of the basin. He looked: staring at the enamel, he saw his blood in scarlet scratches, in indecipherable red networks, in flowing scratches that turned round and round and crossed, intersected, became blurred like illegible constellations beneath him. The star! The yellow star! he thought, there's still that! and he wondered if Bloch would ever forgive him for the nastiness of the Bessières bridge. Then his sisters called to him. He was playing at the back of the garden. He had to come inside for tea. He climbed back upon the terrace with infinite effort, crossing the orchard, leaning his back against the trees to rest, his eyes closed, and he felt the branches moving against his head. Apple trees. They were apple trees, and Simon's titmice were singing in their shining leaves.

He collapsed, let his arms (which now hung against the rim) fall back down, and the blood came forth in thin spurts with surprising speed. Panic-stricken, Jean Calmet tried to straighten up, escape from the trap of that terribly echoing room, call for help, quickly! quickly! He tried to bring his arms back to himself in order to straighten up: impossible. He fell back down. Then tears rolled over his cheeks, his eyes were full of burning salt, he was crying, he was gasping like a desperate child. If he could at least turn off the water! But his arms no longer obeyed. His head fell, the tears mingled with the blood on the enamel, and great sobs now drove violent pains into the back of his throat. He remembered a gathering of good-looking young people, they smiled at him, it was at the Café de l'Évêché, then in a classroom with yellowed walls, he remembered Isabelle growing thin. Then, exhausted, he fell as he would into his grave.

Thus Jean Calmet died.

It had taken him twenty-five minutes.

At La Cité, at the same moment, the examinations for the *bac* were beginning. In haste, they had replaced Jean Calmet; one of the deans had distributed the exam questions in his place and invigilated room 17 from his desk covered with very old ink stains. In the next-to-last row, Marc was already cursing over the translation of Tacitus that Jean Calmet had selected without too much conviction.

One hundred yards from there, Thérèse was waking up in her little room. She was in no hurry. The light filtered through the blinds. The light of June. On the rug, the bedspread rolled into a ball resembled a heap of gold.

In Lutry, Madame Calmet had been up for a long time. She had nibbled a piece of bread, drunk tea, she had done her housework, then she had dressed herself and fixed her hair. Now she was sitting in her armchair, motionless, she looked into the light of the window.

A JEW MUST DIE

Jacques Chessex

A novel based on a true story

On 16 April, 1942, a few days before Hitler's birthday, a handful of
Swiss Nazis in Payerne lure Arthur Bloch, a Jewish cattle merchant,
into a stable and kill him with an iron bar. Europe is in flames but this is
Switzerland and Payerne, a rural market town of butchers and bankers, is
more worried about unemployment and local bankruptcies than the fate
of nations across the border. Fernand Ischi, leader of the local Nazi cell,
blames everything on the Jews and Bloch's murder is to be an example, a
foretaste of what is to come once the Nazis take over Switzerland.

Jacques Chessex, winner of the prestigious Prix Goncourt, is from Payerne. He knew the murderers, went to school with their children. He has
written a taut, implacable story that has awakened memories in a country
that seems to endlessly rediscover dark areas of its past.

PRAISE FOR *A JEW MUST DIE*

**"Told in spare and sober prose, Chessex's final novel is a
masterpiece. A thought-provoking picture of fear and prejudice that will stay with you long after you finish this small but
intensely powerful book."** *The Guardian*

**"In its imagined evocation of historical fact, *A Jew Must Die* is
in itself a justification of the power of art. This brief, disturb-
ing masterpiece goes to the heart of the creative process."**
The Independent

**"It is a swift and stunning narrative based on a true incident.
Read this novel for the history it captures and for the sheer
beauty of its prose."** *Booklist*

£6.99/$12.95/C$14.50
Paperback Original
ISBN 978-1904738-510
eBook
ISBN 978-1904738-572

www.bitterlemonpress.com

THE VAMPIRE OF ROPRAZ

Jacques Chessex

1903, Ropraz, a small village in Switzerland. On a howling December day, a lone walker discovers a recently opened tomb, the body of a young woman violated, her left hand cut off, genitals mutilated and heart carved out. There is horror in the nearby villages: the return of atavistic superstitions and mutual suspicions. Then two more bodies are violated. A suspect must be found. Favez, a stable-boy with blood-shot eyes, is arrested, convicted, placed into psychiatric care. In 1915, he vanishes.

PRAISE FOR *THE VAMPIRE OF ROPRAZ*

"A truly horrifying tale of superstition, madness and retribution. Chessex brilliantly renders both the inhospitable winter landscape of the mountains and the harshness of a society that makes monsters of its victims."
London Review of Books

"In measured prose that studiously sidesteps sensationalism, Chessex recounts the alternating repulsion and fascination of those who vampirically exploit Favez to satisfy their own needs." *Publishers Weekly*

"This is a superb novella by a winner of the Prix Goncourt, written in a spare prose that renders it a thousand times more effective." *The Independent*

'All the more chilling for having its roots in a true story, this is an evocative tale of fear, prejudice and cruelty among country folk." *Daily Mail*

£6.99/$12.95/C$12.95
Paperback Original
ISBN 978-1904738-336
eBook
ISBN 978-1904738-503

www.bitterlemonpress.com